W9-BLE-416

2—

PENGUIN BOOKS

## THE HOUSE ON ECCLES ROAD

Judith Kitchen is the author of two collections of essays, *Only the Dance* and *Distance and Direction*, and the co-editor of two anthologies of creative nonfiction, *In Short* and *In Brief*. She is Writer-in-Residence at SUNY Brockport in upstate New York.

Praise for
*The House on Eccles Road*

**Winner of the S. Mariella Gable Prize
Winner of the Lillian Fairchild Award**

"A definition of a true vision in a novelist is to stride a balance between the novel of the mind and the novel of the heart—exactly the syntheses that Judith Kitchen in *The House on Eccles Road* renders in flawless prose."
      —Stuart Dybck

"When you're reading *The House on Eccles Road*, all you're thinking of is how good a writer Kitchen is and how happy you are to surrender to her way of seeing the world."
      —*The Atlanta Journal-Constitution*

"Poetic and breathtakingly beautiful . . . as the story unfolds, readers witness the intersection of past and present, learning ways that relationships are distorted by memory. Rendered with amazing grace."
      —*Library Journal* (starred)

"This is a mature novel, a novel for grown-ups— where the messiness of a lived life is neither explained or apologized. In beautiful sentence after beautiful sentence, here is Kitchen's vision: abundant and lyrical and true."
　　—Victoria Redel, author of *Loverboy*

A "celebration of Molly's coming of age."
　　—*Publishers Weekly*

"An achingly beautiful novel both of the mind and of the soul, capturing an interior sense that is too fragile to be spoken—too enduring to be broken."
　　—*The North Carolina Sanford Herald*

"At last! A Mollycentric universe. *The House on Eccles Road* is a lovely exploration of history and legacy, with its roots in Dublin and Europe, but it blooms (and Blooms) in our own very mixed-together American air. It's a ripe, rich read."
　　—Albert Goldbarth, author of *Pieces of Payne*

"Rich and compelling . . . it takes chutzpah to attempt a story like this, but in this case, Kitchen succeeds wonderfully."
　　—*Kirkus Reviews*

"I deeply appreciate how [Kitchen] has done what she has done, but most of all I am grateful that she has found a modern way to do an old-fashioned thing: break my heart with words on a page. I bow."
　　—Mary Hood, author of *Familiar Heat*

"Brilliant . . . a famous and somewhat patronized character finally has her say."
　　—*The Women's Review of Books*

# The House on Eccles Road

## *Judith Kitchen*

PENGUIN BOOKS

PENGUIN BOOKS

Published by the Penguin Group
Penguin Group (USA) Inc., 375 Hudson Street,
New York, New York 10014, U.S.A.
Penguin Books Ltd, 80 Strand, London WC2R 0RL, England
Penguin Books Australia Ltd, 250 Camberwell Road,
Camberwell, Victoria 3124, Australia
Penguin Books Canada Ltd, 10 Alcorn Avenue,
Toronto, Ontario, Canada M4V 3B2
Penguin Books India (P) Ltd, 11 Community Centre,
Panchsheel Park, New Delhi – 110 017, India
Penguin Books (N.Z.) Ltd, Cnr Rosedale and Airborne Roads,
Albany, Auckland, New Zealand
Penguin Books (South Africa) (Pty) Ltd, 24 Sturdee Avenue,
Rosebank, Johannesburg 2196, South Africa

Penguin Books Ltd, Registered Offices:
80 Strand, London WC2R 0RL, England

First published in the United States of America by Graywolf Press, 2002
Published in Penguin Books 2003

1  3  5  7  9  10  8  6  4  2

Copyright © Judith Kitchen, 2002
All rights reserved

Excerpt from *Mother Ireland* by Edna O'Brien, copyright © 1976 by Edna
O'Brien. Used by permission of Plume, a division of Penguin Putnam Inc.

THE LIBRARY OF CONGRESS CATALOGING-IN-PUBLICATION DATA
Kitchen, Judith.
The house on Eccles Road / Judith Kitchen.
p.  cm.
ISBN 0 14 20.0330 1 (pbk.)
1. Children—Death—Fiction.   2. College teachers—Fiction.
3. Married people—Fiction.   4. Women singers—Fiction.   5. Grief—Fiction.
I. Title.
PS3561.I845H68  2003
813'.54—dc21   2003042962

Printed in the United States of America
Set in Esprit
Designed by Wendy Holdman

Except in the United States of America, this book is sold subject to the
condition that it shall not, by way of trade or otherwise, be lent, re-sold,
hired out, or otherwise circulated without the publisher's prior consent in
any form of binding or cover other than that in which it is published
and without a similar condition including this condition being
imposed on the subsequent purchaser.

The scanning, uploading and distribution of this book via the Internet
or via any other means without the permission of the publisher is illegal
and punishable by law. Please purchase only authorized electronic editions,
and do not participate in or encourage electronic piracy of copyrighted
materials. Your support of the author's rights is appreciated.

# ACKNOWLEDGMENTS

Seven connected excerpts, taken from Chapters xi, xii, and xiii, were published under the title "Seven Scenes" in *The Atlanta Review,* Fall/Winter 2000.

I am grateful to a fictional character in J. M. Coetzee's essay, "What Is Realism?" first published in *Salmagundi*: "Elizabeth Costello made her name with her fourth novel, *The House on Eccles Street* (1969), whose main character is Marion Bloom, wife of Leopold Bloom, the principal character of another novel, *Ulysses* (1922), by James Joyce." For that idea, I give thanks.

And thanks, too, to the many people who have helped me: Stan Rubin, John Engels, Sharon Bryan, Mary Paumier Jones, Marcia Ullman, George Randels, William, Amanda, Matthew, and Robin. Special thanks to Kit Ward. In memory of Stanley W. Lindberg who encouraged my venture into fiction with great good humor during the last year of his life.

*Hey, little-foot-in-the-sonogram,*
   *this is for you—*
*whoever you will turn out to be*

. . . I want yet again and for indefinable reasons to trace that same route, that trenchant childhood route, in the hope of finding some clue that will, or would, or could, make possible the leap that would restore one to one's original place and state of consciousness, to the radical innocence of the moment just before birth.

—Edna O'Brien, *Mother Ireland*

# THE HOUSE ON ECCLES ROAD

**S**HE WAS NOT GOING TO SPEND the whole day inside, that's one thing she was certain of, though just what she was going to do was vague, as yet unformed, so the day spread itself out like a clean linen tablecloth, waiting for its pleasures, its flatware and candlesticks and bright plaid napkins. No, she was not going to let Leo's failure to mention their anniversary get in the way of her life. Maybe he was going to surprise her this evening, call late in the afternoon and take her off for dinner somewhere in the city. If so, she wondered if he'd come back to pick her up or ask her to come in to join him because then they'd have to take two cars home and neither of them could really drink much wine. These were the kind of details that Leo never thought of. So it would have been better if he'd told her this morning, just before he left, and they might have talked about how to organize their day. But he'd said nothing at all. Not even a question about how she planned to spend her time, and it always bothered her when he didn't seem engaged, and how often had she told him that, so that now it began to feel deliberate, though if she were honest, she knew it wasn't really deliberate, but certainly thoughtless even so.

She hated June, really. Such an indeterminate month. Not the small mouthings of April, the leaves unfurling all chartreuse and newly minted. Or the mild, blowsy rapture of May. No, June turned hot and everything was overgreen and the days had a kind of sameness that she didn't remember being part of any other time of the year. They should have been married in October, under a clear blue sky, the leaves a chatter of color. They should have been married in December, a few flakes falling and darkness descending in the middle of the afternoon so that all the interiors looked warm and inviting. They should have been married at the end of August when the fields have gone dusty and time itself is a haze on the horizon. June was so unoriginal. Everything in her life had turned out to be ordinary, or almost ordinary. Yet she'd had her own passions, her griefs, so why did they seem, today, like husks of someone else's emotions?

She'd stood at the top of the stairs, waiting to hear him say, "Molly? Listen, Mol, what should we do tonight to celebrate?" And instead she'd heard the garage doors opening and his car sliding out into daylight. There, through the window, a sheen of sun on the hood so it didn't look black, but green, like a pond dappled in sunlight, drenched, but also the hard glint of metal, something hardened like the shell of a beetle, something enclosing him and taking him off. He didn't have to be going, but he was. He didn't have to teach all summer, but he'd elected to do this two-month course, keeping her here in exile from her beloved coast, and for what, for a couple of thousand extra dollars they didn't really need? No, it was so he wouldn't have time to think. He always avoided time to think—the very thing she craved and coddled. She was a solitary creature, she guessed, in the way she liked their summers away, tucked into the tiny kitchen and front deck overlooking the ocean, watching the lobster boats make their daily rounds like an irregular clock. She liked the way she was quiet then, talking mostly to the woman at the post office or the girl behind the counter at the deli, passing the time of day and then leaving again for the company of her own thoughts. She couldn't tell you what she was thinking those long afternoons when the light seemed to splay itself out on the surface of the water, but there was a lifting of sorrow, a sense that she belonged to something larger than her own troubles. Maybe she was thinking about nothing, simply absorbing the light and the sound of the waves on the rocks the way her body absorbed the sweet buttery lobster they cracked open with their hands at Robinson's Wharf. Gulls would swoop down for the pickings, or stand on the pilings, brazen and belligerent, their eyes like beads of determination, and the two of them would laugh, then, caught in the moment, everything that had gone before frozen in the winter they'd left behind.

Leo looked younger on those summer piers, less worried by whatever it was that worried him. At home he was often disheveled, scattered about the house as though pieces of him were fluttering away. A confetti of obligations. Nothing quite finished. He was forever picking up strays—kittens and hurt birds and, most of all, the type of student who would never amount to much of anything but seemed to need something to hold onto. Leo took them under his wing, briefly, before they abandoned him in search of someone more controlling, someone they could eventually resist. So over the years there had been a succession of angry young men in search of an object for their anger and Leo worrying about what would become of them. It had gone on long enough that she could recount what had become of them: one lawyer, two salesmen, someone with an indefinite job in computers, a third-grade teacher, a halfhearted musician, and two who had simply dropped out of sight. And some who were still in the making.

Today he'd looked old. Or at least tired. And the sun had broken over the hood of his car until it disappeared in dazzle. And he'd backed down the driveway and turned toward the city and left her standing on the upstairs landing with a day to fill, and a night, and he was off to his appointed rounds as though she were so far from his thoughts that her figure on the stairs would dissolve into the sunlight and she would simply be another part of the physical reality of his day. A dust mote floating in the lit space above the rug.

And Leo, backing out of the driveway, glanced up once to see her standing there, looking down. At least it looked as though she were looking down, though it was hard to tell because he had to squint into the splashed glass, and then he had to turn back to the steering wheel and the rearview mirror to see if any cars were coming down Larch Lane. He hadn't gotten used to calling it Larch Lane even though that had been its name for the past five years. Their house was an old farmhouse, completely remodeled, but he remembered when it stood alone on this road and the fields across from it chronicled the seasons. And then the farmer had sold his fields and the contractor had come and suddenly all the streets were named for trees. Linden and Poplar and Chestnut and Larch. Funny, there wasn't an Oak, yet oaks were really the only trees around, except for the fancier little red-leaved decorations their neighbors seemed to prefer, or the flowering crab apples, things that didn't produce fruit or shade as far as he could tell.

There was probably something he'd forgotten. There was always something he'd forgotten, but he'd grown used to that feeling, the feeling that nothing was complete. Nothing squared and easy. Nothing like a city block, something you could go around and come back to where you started. Here you could get lost in the twists of Poplar Road and never come back to its intersection with Larch. The land had been tamed, but not in an orderly fashion. He'd have loved some logic. Even the logic of his childhood where 27th followed 26th and East or West told you which side of the city you were headed for. He did not have a mind for suburbia and he hadn't chosen to be a part of it. It had caught up with him one September afternoon when the field was a whispering stand of drying corn stubble and four yellow backhoes had come out of nowhere to dig cellar holes and smooth out the outline of a street.

Nothing in his life was quite the way he'd planned it, if wanting could be called a plan. He supposed it couldn't, because you'd have to decide how to go about getting what you wanted, and he hadn't really figured out how to do that. It was lucky he could teach, because there wasn't much else he was suited for. And there was the occasional bright eye somewhere near the back of the room that told him he'd said something that spoke directly to the heart. That kept him going, he thought, that, or the thought that it might happen next time. And he was talking about what he loved most in the world, or almost most, and that was somehow good, wasn't it? Because nothing had seemed very good for the past eight years and that wasn't really fair, was it, because there were good things but they paled beside his dreams deferred. So when he looked up and saw her there he didn't know what was in her mind, whether she wanted something from him that he'd forgotten how to give, or whether she was counting out the loads of laundry she'd need to do before lunch or dreaming of the place on the coast they'd go to for only the month of August this year, or whether she was standing, as she sometimes did, with a blank look on her face that could be read as repose or bereavement and he didn't dare break into that look because he wasn't sure which he'd rather she was feeling.

He'd have to call Marcie, his daughter. She was causing them no end of trouble and he really didn't know what to do about it. It wasn't as though he could do much since she hadn't lived with him since she was twelve and she certainly gave him no authority. But she seemed to have an idea of what he owed her that transcended even the boundaries of his guilt. He wasn't guilty, not really, of a divorce that had been inevitable and not even of his choosing. He wished he had chosen it, wished he had been the one to call everything off—action-packed anger—because it was worth calling it off and his own suffering would at least have come to fruition. But instead Sarah had been the one to serve him with papers, served him in public so that he felt lit from within, exposed, and therefore all the more reluctant. Let her take me to trial, he'd thought, and dug in his heels, though it had left him without money. So it would be hard to send any to Marcie now because he was only just recovering, fourteen years later, from those horrendous debts. And she was saying he owed it to her, which sounded, somehow, just like her mother, and he wasn't happy seeing her mother in her because this was the girl he'd read to every night and now her voice held the tinge of contempt he'd heard from before her birth and she was almost a stranger, this being he'd watched sleeping in her bed feeling his heart fill with emotion he couldn't name, but it had extended out into the future and seemed to assuage every hardship endured by great-great-grandparents whose names he didn't even know as they labored in the villages of Russia. She was the future, and now she called from her first year in graduate school and talked about his duty, when he'd done his duty and where it had led him was into a darkness he didn't want to think about.

He was doing his duty now, driving off to his office hours where he would counsel that young man, Steve, who had it in him to become something special. He knew it, had seen it in his blazing eyes the day before, had seen the list of books he was reading and the way he was putting them together, casting off his old Catholicism in favor of literature with the fatalism of the truly converted. Steve would go on to do what Leo had never done: he'd right the wrongs by force of will. Leo could feel it as the car turned toward the magnet of the city. He could feel himself snap awake. Alert, as in the old days, as when he had thought that life did make sense and that he was a small part of it.

How small the car becomes so quickly, Molly thought, as it rounded the curve, disappeared, then came into view for a final instant before it took on a life of its own. Distance and size, equally abstract. So that if you went far enough away from your problems they, too, would shrink. Or would they simply come along, magnified in the unfamiliarity of some new place? She'd only gone back to the coast, to the familiar, and things there had stayed exactly as large or as small as they'd ever been. But memory, memory had a way of letting things grow larger without becoming more threatening. She could go back to her childhood so easily, really, a flick of the wrist and she was able to call it all up. The heavy front door and the cool hallway where the sepia stares of her great-grandparents looked down from either side of the wavery mirror. Her mother somewhere in the kitchen and her father about to return from work. The house filled with expectation. She and Brian were free to do what they needed. Sometimes she'd envied him his dogged persistence, the way he spent hour after hour on his airplane models or sorting his baseball cards. She'd done nothing, really, except dream her time away, her mind like a fox darting into its hole, probing through the mist of dream for something that would make her respond. She could remember the exact feeling of being in her room doing nothing, absolutely nothing, but knowing that someday she would do something and that it would have meaning. She could remember her eyes in the mirror and the dusting of powder on the vanity and the blouses all ironed and hung on their hangers and the pink plastic radio with Johnny Mathis on her favorite station and the afternoon closing down all around her and her eyes looking as though the fire were banked, ready to burst into flame if someone blew on it. And then the front door would open and close, her father's voice at the bottom of the stairs, and the family would fall into place and she could come down to be part of its wholeness.

So Molly knew what she was missing when she

watched the last dark flicker of the car between the trees, and she knew what had happened to her life as it snagged on its lack of direction. And she wasn't going to spend the whole day of her thirteenth anniversary (actually her second thirteenth anniversary, if she were to be exact) playing house in the house she had chosen. Because Molly hadn't chosen all the vinyl-sided neighbors with their cathedral ceilings and their Japanese maples or the way her sense of the land had been wrested from her so that now she could not look out her window and call up her childhood. The very fact that she needed a car of her own—that they were of two-car status—told her everything she needed to know. She was free to do as she pleased, and she didn't know what would please her.

June did not please her, not here, in this heat. She wanted the ocean, its dotting of islands, and a lighthouse throwing its lonely light across the bay. She wanted to feel the way she had when she was twenty, as though the world were glowing, and even the dirt on the sidewalk took on a distinction, as if she had simply put on a new pair of glasses and everything danced up, finite and unutterably beautiful. She wanted to walk the streets of New York filled with the excitement she'd felt then, the crowds that pushed her out of the way and the strange little corner eateries with their Formica counters and yellow Naugahyde stools, the smell of hot pastrami permeating the sidewalks, rising a little, like a haze over the streets. And night coming on in the city, the buildings lit like hives, until she could almost hear the humming bustle of people coming home, unlocking their doors, the click of heels on hardwood, the clink of ice in glasses and then the slow easing out of the day into the rituals of evening. The steady concentration of chopping boards all over the city, the onions and carrots and lettuce of millions filling the salad bowls to overflowing as the city drank in the daylight sounds and muffled them under its pillows. Then the long light of evening as taxis geared up for another rush to the playhouses and nightclubs, cut through by the wail of a siren on a side street, something to make you think of other lives, other dramas you would never see or know. The rattle of the subway under the pavement, a blur of sound, then the relative silence of its absence. And all of it bound up with being twenty, eyes still fresh from her small hometown, wanting to take it in and keep it there, like a bird in a cage, so she might have it later—now—to say this, this is what I have been longing for. This past, so ephemeral, so completely realized in a body grown tired of its company.

No, Molly was tired of her own realized dreams. Her house with its wide pine boards and its linen closet. Her car, bright red, as though it could cheer her up merely to start the ignition. Her sense of herself as caught somewhere between what she might have been and what she had become. She didn't recognize herself in the mirror these mornings, saw, instead, her face at sixteen, backed by the pink-flowered wallpaper of her childhood bedroom, her hair refusing to curl up in the fashion of the day and the whole day ruined by its refusal. She saw herself as just beginning something when, really, she was at the cusp of winding down. Her thirteenth anniversary with Leo, her second husband, and the leaves spread wide over their garden, dropping their shade like cold evidence of the darkness at the center. Her lawn under a wide green awning to cover the day's beginnings. If she looked up, Leo's car would be long gone and she would be left to decide, once again, her own direction.

**S**HE WAS HUMMING A LITTLE AS she washed and combed her hair, an old Irish tune she vaguely remembered from one of her uncles. She knew so many Irish songs, their progressions like a recipe for grief. She'd been so young when she learned them that their words hadn't meant much to her, she'd just liked the way the high notes rose and shimmered. And then, quite suddenly it seemed, there had been the world of voice lessons—music to be read rather than felt—and she'd been so confused. Songs were for the mood of the moment and yet in college she was asked to sing on cue, asked to read what looked for all the world like a foreign language, nothing that connected her life to the sound she was supposed to be making.

From then on, music had seemed somehow alien, residing outside the body, something to study, but nothing minted in the heart. And she'd been successful, she supposed, making a modest living by doing what she loved. But she didn't love it, really, not the way she had loved hearing her uncles suddenly break into song, then slide back to their stories, as though the two were connected by the thinnest of membranes. The tune would carry the longing back through the years and revive it, sung as though to her. That was music, that spontaneity, that sorrow refined to one held note resting in the palm of the hand. But what she did was singing, which wasn't always the same thing as music, no matter what others thought.

So the tune surprised her, seemed to come from somewhere so deep within that she could barely remember the girl she had been, could not call up the time when it settled inside her like a rabbit in its hutch. And now here it was, this was a gift from the past, this scrap of tune that connected her to her father and her father's brothers, James and Terry. Which one had sung it for her first, and where had he first heard it? Probably from their father who had come from Ireland, a small town between Killarney and Killorglin called Beaufort. Beautiful fort. An infinitesimal dot on the map. When she'd gone there five summers ago, she'd found only two pubs, a grocery, a post office, and a scattering of houses. No fort that she could see, and nothing very beautiful. Or else everything so beautiful it felt commonplace. There was a new spackled house with insulated windows on the land where her grandfather had grown up, so she'd had to imagine the tiny three-room cottage where he'd slept four to a bed and started off for school with a hot potato in his pocket. Which were the only stories she could remember his telling her before he died and slipped into that place where memory and imagination coincide. So it felt as though she were being visited by hovering mountains and stony lakes, by the sight of a Celtic cross in the tiny graveyard on the hill, by a field with two spotted ponies, or a painted cart full of gypsies, any or all of the sights she had taken in because they might have been seen by him as well.

What were the words? She could remember one phrase only, something about a stinging nettle, and even that seemed wrong, as though she were remembering badly something she had misunderstood at the time. She'd try to look up that song in the music library at the university. But not yet. For now, it would retain its magic by coming unbidden, a fragment from childhood, still a part of the freedom it would lose as soon as it had a title, the barred rigor that robbed it of its irrepressible grace notes. But what were the words? She could almost hear Terry's voice, wavering, trying to pick them out of his past. Or was it James?

All that seemed so long ago, when they'd climb out of their old grey Chevrolet to help her father cut up the huge tree that had landed in their yard during the flood. And the flood itself seemed like a dream. A five-year-old's dream where things swirl and mix and nothing is ordinary.

So when the phone rang Molly was humming and she really wanted to get to the end before she answered, so she let the phone ring four times before she picked it up and heard Marcie saying, "Where's my dad?" without so much as a "hello" or a "how are you?" which always unnerved her. It wasn't as though she hadn't spent countless weekends trying to please the girl, letting her have friends over to sleep, cooking them meals, driving them to the drugstore for nail polish and hair coloring and all the things that made no sense to her but seemed to make sense to them. It wasn't as though she hadn't spent time picking out gifts—the silver earrings from Ireland and the polished black pottery from the Southwest—that she thought Marcie would like. But to Marcie she still didn't count as a person, and it was beginning to wear thin. She'd been waiting for something to happen, for Marcie to realize that she was someone with a life of her own, feelings and ambitions and preferences. Waiting for maturity to catch her up and she was old enough now, god knows, to begin the two-way street of adult relationships, but still there was that demanding edge in her voice, that dismissive tone that wanted only her father.

"He's teaching this summer. You know that." But Marcie didn't seem to know, Molly thought, only to know that she wanted something now and that he ought to be there when she wanted to talk. Did she realize that Leo, too, was a person, that the money came from his long hours at the office, the countless papers he read and graded, the committees and meetings and long-winded lectures. He might live a rarefied life, but it had its own rigors and its rhythms. When would Marcie understand that?

And Marcie, impatient and wanting to get on with her day, didn't really want to spend time making small talk with Molly, who struck her as just a bit too desperate to hear what she wished to hear. And she wasn't going to tell her things she didn't feel, just because Molly had wanted her to say them for longer than she cared to remember. Wanted Marcie to be effusive in her thanks, or to go on and on about those silver earrings and they were nice, but really, it's not as though you couldn't get earrings everywhere. It wasn't *her* grandfather who had come from Ireland, so why should it matter so much. They were nice, but she'd rather have money, at least at this moment, so maybe she'd like them better in the future when she had enough other things. Maybe she'd pick them up someday, hold them up to her ears in the mirror, and think about Molly and Dad leaning over the counter in a little Irish shop, holding up pair after pair and thinking of her, but for now, she didn't want them to think of her, or not that way.

Not that she knew what she wanted from them. Time, she guessed. Though she'd turned down the invitation to come to Maine. Maine was nice, too, but it had been nicer when she was fourteen and hadn't cared that there wasn't very much to do. She'd been able to get a good tan by lying out on the rocks, and the ocean was exciting, crashing and crashing until its rhythm was part of her blood. By the next summer it had seemed boring, except when they went into town where a group of six boys always seemed to be hanging around the deli, just outside around one of the old picnic tables where they seemed to pile up an endless number of empty root-beer bottles. They always whistled or laughed or made silly comments and one of them usually tugged at her ponytail and she could spin around and act insulted, stamp her foot to make them laugh harder. Molly had smiled, as though she knew how she felt, but she didn't. No one knew how she felt to be stuck in Maine when her friends in Boston were all hanging out at the record store or going to the movies. Who wanted to go on another whale watch? Or that stupid, silly circus that came every year to Damariscotta? She was far too old for the circus and yet Dad and Molly seemed to be having so much fun. She couldn't stand the way they liked those elephants who were doing the twist. It was so corny. And they seemed to think it was so funny. Though they probably did remember doing the twist themselves. She couldn't imagine that. They were so old and stodgy, hard to think of them letting their bodies go that way, almost as sickening to think of them as to watch the shapeless folds of those elephants, the skin hanging down and shaking a bit as they rotated their back legs, making their butts swivel, as if they could hear the music and respond, which she highly doubted.

And she'd forgotten that her father was teaching,

though, if she thought about it, that's the only reason for her to be calling them at home instead of in Maine, so it had been partly in her mind. She needed to know if he was going to help her out because she'd been invited to the Cape for three weeks at the end of the summer and if he was going to give her some money then she could quit the stupid job at the pizza parlor early, though she wouldn't tell her boss yet because then he wouldn't have any commitment to her and she needed the work for a while. But she needed to know or she might not be able to say yes and she wanted to say yes, but of course she would say yes even if she hadn't talked to her dad because she'd find a way, she always found a way. It was just so hard to have to say something to *her* before she could hang up. Why wouldn't Molly just tell her he wasn't there and then hang up? Why did her voice always sound like a question mark at the other end? It would be nice not to always feel that Molly wanted something.

It wasn't coming, Molly could sense that. She wanted some change in tone, some sense of recognition. Marcie was simply not growing up. Was hanging up now, telling her to have her dad call between six and seven because that's when she'd be home. But Molly didn't know where they would be between six and seven, or even if they'd talk to each other before that. Not a word about their anniversary, which she supposed Marcie did not celebrate, but still, she might realize that they might be celebrating, if, indeed, they were. But since she didn't even know that, she couldn't use it as a kind of reminder, couldn't say, "Well, he won't be able to call then because we're eating out for our anniversary," one of those sentences that made you feel both better and worse for having said it. Better because part of you wanted to make her recognize your marriage. Worse because she'd gotten to you enough to make you want that.

So Molly said nothing but, "I'll let him know you want to talk," and then she hung up the phone, its white plastic world, its intrusion. The song all but lost in the flood of feelings that Marcie stirred. She was sure that if she'd had a daughter of her own things would be different, but of course she'd seen enough of mothers and daughters to know better. Still, Molly would have been so happy. Something good would have come of it, at least by the time her child was twenty-six. Though her own daughter would have been much younger than that, probably sulking about having to go to Maine and being a pain about everything. And even that was silly, because she'd never had a daughter, only a vague and fleeting dream until the baby was born and then she never thought about it again. Her son would have understood her. She pushed that thought aside, or tried to, because she couldn't help comparing Leo's living daughter with her own dead son, and all it did was feed her anguish. He'd have been twelve. He'd have hated going to Maine, too, wanting to stay with his soccer team for the last seven games of the season. Or saying that all there was to do was fish for crabs, or stare at the stupid tide pools, nothing exciting. And she'd remember how he'd been when he was eight, loving the tide pools, spending hours watching the anemones and the little water creatures and sometimes building little islands of sand for them and waiting for the tide to creep slowly in and cover the world he'd created. Or how he'd sit on the pier, peering down into the water beneath, watching for some sign of movement at the end of his line. The shout as he hauled up crab after crab; their pincers; how he'd always wanted her to help him throw them back. But he'd never been eight. Never been old enough to fish for crabs. So why did she bring him to life in these ways, as though he had a shadow life, a chronology, a perfection in the imagination that did not stop on that day eight years ago when his breathing had stopped? That walked out of the hospital room and into the blue sky of a future he never would have.

There was no use thinking of all of this even though she knew enough to know that you can't help thinking about what comes to mind when you haven't planned to think it. She wasn't dwelling on the past as Leo called it, at least that's not how she saw it, when it surfaced as part of the present. She was shouldering the past because it was there. It was real, and you couldn't simply wish it away, even though Leo seemed to try to handle it that way. She didn't think that Leo had really handled anything, simply had put it aside and pretended to go on living until the pretense was as solid as anything else in his life. She supposed their friends would say he'd managed better than she had. Gone on with his job, made things happen. And she'd simply retreated. Though she thought of those two years when she spent most of her time fixing the house, not answering the phone, not returning calls, as part of what she needed to do. There were so many things she needed to do, and one of them was to paint the woodwork. Or design the skylight that made all the difference in the room where Leo wrote. She needed to pull her life together and tie the knot, tie it in place, tie it to this place, this house on Eccles Road, though that had been about to change and soon even the name of her road had been pulled out from under her, but meanwhile she needed to make something beautiful in her life because she couldn't sing and her songs had always been the most beautiful thing about her.

When music deserted her, it had felt like someone else had died. Someone inside her. Simply disappeared. She'd felt as though she needed to sit still and quiet to wait for her songs to return. And they didn't come. The months became a year, and she couldn't bear to hear a fiddle. Her throat would tighten into a lump and she would swallow and swallow, trying not to let the tears that seemed just beneath the surface brim over. Trying not to let Leo see that she was so soft, so completely undone. It would mean that their life together was not enough, and it was, had been. But it had been altered and then altered again, and they were not the same two people who had begun it all. They were different and they didn't dare to look at each other. Or rather, she hadn't dared to look at him pretending, and he'd pretended to look at her but he wasn't actually looking, only glancing in her direction, not looking, because looking would have meant that he understood that the songs had disappeared and he'd have held her and cried and cried for her songs until one of them flew into her mouth, a croon to tell him it would never be over, but it would be all right. And if he had looked, maybe it would have been all right, but she couldn't know that now, because he'd only glanced, and the song had turned hard and glittery in its shell, resisting the words that might connect it with what she was feeling.

**S**HE WAS NOT GOING TO SPEND the day thinking about the past, that's for sure. There had to be something she needed to do, something that would get her outside, at least into the air-conditioned car where she wouldn't feel as though all she wanted to do was lie down and wait for evening when a breeze would pick up. She liked the way the car insulated her from everything, made things appear closer and more available as she sped past. She had choices, though. She could turn away from the city, away from the village of Dublin, too, all the malls and developments, drive until the houses thinned and the road meandered on the way toward the next town. Not the highway, but a two-lane road that used to be the main artery across the state. Now it was lined with crumbling gas stations and the few stores that had become antique shops. People from the city came on weekends, hoping for a bargain. And off that road there were others, badly paved, that wound south into the hills that would, eventually, lead to Sinking Spring and the hills of her childhood. She felt at home in them, in their unthinking presence, in the shadows that held the valleys like mysterious folds. She liked the tops of the hills best, where farmers had staked a claim and now held on fiercely. You'd drive through forest and then emerge in another world where corn and wheat made a patchwork and the old tractors littered the farmyards. Once in a while there was a dairy and the cows spread their blacks and whites up and down the uneven landscape. But she wouldn't go that way, not today, because it might make her sad to be so happy. She knew that didn't make sense, but it did to her, and today she wanted to be happy to be happy. She'd go into the city and, sometime in the afternoon, she'd try to reach Leo and by then maybe he'd remember to ask her about dinner and they could make some plans. She wasn't cooking tonight, not on her anniversary, no matter what. Or maybe she ought to be prepared, ought to surprise him with something nice, take the initiative.

Her car was her companion, that's what she felt as she pulled out quickly and headed to the market. She knew her car better than she knew her friends. And it knew her, knew enough to meld itself to her moods. Knew her songs from deep inside so they filled the interior with something bittersweet. Knew her quick hops to punctuate the day and her long, time-consuming drives in aimless circles through the countryside. Knew how to read her mind, turning left at the bottom of the driveway and giving a quick toot to her neighbor across the street, out watering her lawn before the sun got too high. Jackie was pregnant again and Molly was happy for her, though how she would handle three small kids was beyond her. Jackie pretended to be happy, Molly knew, because she'd told her, but she really had wanted to go back to school and earn her degree in business. They needed the money, and the boys were almost ready for school full-time. And now this.

Five more years of diapers and fevers and mopping up spills and watching someone else learn to talk and then having to talk to it, read to it, make it responsible for what it was doing, Jackie was thinking. She could call it her, since she knew it was going to be a girl from the sonogram, but she wished she didn't know that. She hadn't known with either of her boys and they'd been fine. Now she didn't even have to choose a boy's name and that seemed sad, as though her imagination had been cut in half, and she was forced to look at all the little dresses in the fancy shop in the village and think only of Lynnie this and Lynnie that, making her a person before she even came into this world and that seemed so terrifying she preferred to think of her as "it" in case she could ward off bad luck.

She'd heard about Molly's boy, though not from Molly. You'd never know he'd existed except for the photo on their mantel, a boy about three, blond, with a tinge of red in his hair, and bright, dark eyes. By now his hair would probably have been darker, gone brown the way hair does, but in the picture it looked like spun gold. Molly never told her about him, not even after her two boys were born. And now she was tooting her horn as she drove off, friendly as always, but really not as involved a neighbor as Leo. Leo would come over to talk to her some evenings when she was sitting in the lawn chair, trying to stay cool, and she'd told Leo that the baby was going to be a girl, that they'd probably name her Lynne. He'd seemed so interested in how they knew, saying that he couldn't get over what had happened in science in his own lifetime. Now they could save people who had died of awful diseases just a few years before. And she had grown quiet, knowing that they'd made so many strides against lymphoma in the past eight years that that thought couldn't help but be going through his head. Leo was able to face his life, Jackie thought, and Molly always seemed to be skittish, not quite there, not in the best sense of the word. Molly reminded her of a bird. In a cage. Almost friendly, but if you left the door open, she'd fly out and be gone. Maybe she'd hover in a nearby tree, but always in a branch just out of reach, like those parakeets she'd read about somewhere in Brooklyn, lost pets that eluded everyone and had formed another life on their own. She wondered how parakeets could survive the winters, but probably in the city there were places near steam vents, or something, places where they could stay warm. She wondered why they didn't migrate south to look for the equivalent of their original home in the jungles. They didn't have the instincts, she guessed, wincing as she bent over to adjust the hose and the baby kicked, or was it a contraction? If it was, it was probably nothing, because there were three weeks left to go. She'd never have another baby in July, that's for sure. She'd never have another baby at all if she could help it, and women could help it now, not like fifty years ago when you had to take what life handed you. Sorry, Lynne, she thought, I'll want you when I see you, but right now you seem like five years of endlessness.

In the rearview mirror, Molly saw Jackie bend down to tug at the hose and thought how truly beautiful the pregnant body is in its slow awkwardness. How all the movements seem deliberate and carefully planned, as though the flesh wanted to conserve all its energy for what it was about to endure. She wondered whether Jackie wanted a girl or a boy, a girl probably with two boys already, though sometimes people were practical and wanted to be able to use the clothes they already had, things like that. Or planned how the boys could share a bedroom, but Jackie's house had four bedrooms, so there was no problem there unless they needed a spare room, parents coming to visit, that sort of thing. But Jackie's parents came every other year from Seattle, so it wasn't as though they saw them all that often, and Bob's parents seemed so feeble the couple of times Molly had met them. They didn't seem to register this new young family as an extension of themselves, but as strangers they happened to have Thanksgiving dinner with, all that noise and fuss and bother and for what? And then Jackie was out of sight behind the other houses on the curve and Molly was heading for the market where she could stock up on something just in case.

The market pleased her. It was small and exclusive, with fresh vegetables and meats, special pastas, extra virgin olive oil, all the specialties of suburban America. She had wanted to despise it when it appeared, built almost overnight, flimsy and superficial. But the manager was so pleasant and his taste so right that she'd been won over. She loved the fact that they carried local produce and the way everything seemed to shine. Vinegars in long rows near the window so that the colors ranged from clear to ochre to the palest of pinks with an herb swirling in its depths. She'd buy that ginger pasta Leo loved. And smoked salmon. Avocado or melon. Too bad it was so early in the growing season. The tomatoes would taste like wood. Better to do without, find a range of greens, some summer squash. Endive for the salad. And fresh oranges. It was nice to have a market like this one so she didn't have to drive the extra miles to the supermarket and stand in long lines while people cashed out their coupons. She did that once a month, and she knew it was less expensive, but it was less pleasant. And part of what she wanted to pay for was the pleasure of fresh sole or tiny two-person bunches of parsley. Not the wholesale boxes of detergent and cereal that she couldn't even find a place to fit on their shelves. Maybe she was old-fashioned, but she liked the smaller sizes, the cycle of replenishment.

So she smiled at Lucy behind the checkout counter.

Lucy had become a kind of friend, at least someone you could tell a bit about yourself. That's because Lucy was also trying to become an actress and had once asked Molly's opinion about trying out for the local summer theater. Go for it, she'd told her, because who knows? There's always a part that's just right for someone, and maybe it will be you. You have to trust your talents. Though Molly didn't trust her own, not anymore, not after that night eight years ago when the baby-sitter had called about Arjay. Fever, she'd said. And shivering. And Molly had told her to give him two baby aspirins and she'd be home after the performance, but she really couldn't come right then, she was due onstage any minute. It was only a musical at the local high school, running for five nights, but Molly had known the songs were hers to sing, that they spoke for her. She couldn't really act, but the songs would carry her, she thought, and actually the songs had turned her into Evita, so that she found herself acting in spite of herself. Don't cry for me, she had belted out, and her voice expanded, a contralto whose range covered the pampas and the forests of her country. She'd loved that part so much. Not that she could have saved him if she'd rushed right home. No, that was only the beginning of doctors and specialists and months of trying to find out what was wrong and then knowing what was wrong and trying to find the specialist who could save him. One doctor so arrogant she felt he would cheat his own children at Monopoly, but then, that's who you wanted on your side, didn't you? Didn't you? Painful, horrible, nasty months in which hope bounced in like a ball every time the phone rang, then disappeared with each new test. Poor little Arjay pricked and poked and growing thinner and thinner, as though he might simply slip away from them. His strange passivity. Growing old before his time, with that strange wisdom of children who are ill and know it. His little eyes gone solemn until she could hardly bear to look at him for what they told her.

And Lucy smiled back, telling Molly she had something to ask her. Did she want to come with her to audition for the musical this year? She'd heard they needed someone middle-aged, with a voice that could stop the show. And Lucy didn't know of anyone else who fit that description. Not that Lucy had ever heard Molly sing, but she'd heard people talk about Molly singing. Like an angel, one woman had said. No, not an angel, said another, like an oboe. Her voice floated out over the audience as though it came from somewhere else. And another time a man told her he'd heard her sing at weddings and it made him cry every time, even when he wasn't emotionally involved in who was getting married. She was that good, he'd said. So Lucy wondered . . .

And Molly looked up, surprised. Surprised that no one had asked this obvious question for years. They'd stopped asking. Stopped trying to bring her out of herself. And here was Lucy who didn't share her history, asking her a simple question. And yes, Molly said, yes, I'd love to. Because she would love to, she realized, she would love to sing and be whole again. Would love to give life to every dead bone in her body. Yes, she said, yes.

She'd stop at the mall after all. She hated the mall, but she'd pick up something for Jackie's baby. Yellow, she guessed, to be safe. A quilt. Because by now all the blankets would have been used up by the boys and it was nice to have the bed look new, as though in those weeks just before birth there was a sense of someone already there, and the quilt would feel anticipatory. She hated the mall, the rows and rows of parked cars so that you had to memorize where yours was and even then you got all turned around and came out the wrong door and your car was not where you'd left it. Someone had told her to notice what kind of car was parked next to yours, but she thought that didn't make sense because the car might leave, and besides she didn't ever recognize the make of cars, they looked like cars to her, basically the same shape, not the same color. Once she had parked next to a pickup truck and then she'd noticed the man coming back to it. He looked right past her car to the one next to it, looking the car over and over, so she glanced to her right and there was a small red convertible. When she got out, she memorized the kind of car that was: Triumph. It had two tiny British flags painted on its side. But she'd never seen another car like that. And the pickup, she remembered, was a beat-up beige, maybe a Ranger, but she wouldn't swear to it. She loved to hate the mall. She hated the shops, the same shops all over America, so that every baby was dressed in Baby Gap and every farm boy in north Georgia could wear a pair of Reeboks, or whatever happened to be the latest style. The fluorescent lights made everything go bright, shimmery, and the colors artificial, until the whole of America glared in the false light of desire. Old women sat at tables in the middle of an air-conditioned food mall, Styrofoam cups of coffee and plastic stirrers for their synthetic cream, and around them swirled the startling sounds of a merry-go-round. An indoor carousel, with plastic molded horses and a tinny sound. Spinning out the fake magic of a day on the town. So she hurried past what would, in her day, have been the record shops but now held rows and rows of CDs in their impossible cellophane wrappings, past the leather shops and the earring store where, for ten dollars, you could have your ears (or other parts) pierced, past the appliance store with its banks of TV sets all tuned to the same station, a tic-tac-toe of faces, some redder or greener than others, all moving in unison. Into and out of, not like the teenagers who used the mall like a second home, a place to hang out. Or the walking aimless, those with nothing to do and time on their hands. Into and out of, except that it was hard to find a yellow quilt—everything shocking pink or turquoise and covered in cute designs of cartoon characters—and Molly wanted plain and simple, no, plain and elegant, and it took three stores to find it. And no place in its right mind should have three stores with baby quilts, except that it was probably good, wasn't it, to be able to have the choices? Though she wasn't sure. The mall made her feel ambivalent.

It made her feel that maybe her taste was wrong and she was old-fashioned and somewhat stodgy. Something wrong with her, she was thinking, because she couldn't eat out in the middle of a sea of shoppers at a wobbly wrought-iron table under a falsely cool sky filled with plastic trees.

Yet part of her was secretly intrigued by the life of the mall, the people who felt at home there and seemed to know what they were doing. Part of her was drawn to the cave-like interiors of the stores, the glittering mirrors that doubled and tripled the seductive rows of dresses or slacks. The kitchenware outlet where she could spend an hour mulling over vegetable peelers or expensive coffeemakers or just admiring the shape and color of a salad bowl. Part of her felt as though it could live in the mall forever, in its rarefied air of optimism and goodwill. She hated to love the mall, but there it was, she had to admit it.

So she blinked as she entered daylight again, even though, in reality, it was probably less bright outside than in. Blinked herself back into a world where sunlight made the tiny green leaves on the hedgerow give up a hint of the red they would later become and where the blast of hot air could make you go limp in its wake. Looking for a red car parked somewhere between E-16 and E-17, on a bright morning in June when, by all rights, people should be watering their gardens or riding bicycles lazily up and down the streets and were, instead, parked next to her in aisle E and now off somewhere in never-never land looking for their own equivalent of a yellow quilt.

**S**TRANGE, SHE WAS THINKING, how we go through our lives on remote control. She couldn't remember putting the bags in the car, or turning the key, or heading back toward her house, but here she was on Eccles Road, sorry, on Larch, winding her way back toward her own asphalt driveway. Of course, the groceries should go in the refrigerator, then they'd be here in case. She could use the new turquoise candles and have dinner on the side porch. It would be cool enough by then, and she could use that green glass lantern she'd bought last year and never taken out of the box. They could raise their glasses of wine and drink to the future, and maybe they would both sense a future that didn't depend on what they couldn't have.

That'll be Leo, she thought, when the phone rang. Its shrill, insistent sound, as though it were issuing a command. He had remembered. But no, it wasn't Leo at all, but a voice from the past, saying something as corny as, "Here is a voice from your past." But she was pleased, truly pleased, to hear Ted Boyle's voice. So long ago. "Lucy just told me the good news." Lucy? Oh, yes, Lucy, the girl in the market. What news? Oh, yes, that she'd audition for the musical. It seemed like something from another life. And his voice was from another life, from before, from when he was the director and she was singing and her life stretched out before her and he had been so attentive, so much a part of it. And now here he was again, talking as though they had talked these last few years, as lightly and easily as they always talked. How good it would be to see her, how he thought of her over and over, how he wondered what she was doing, how good it was to hear from Lucy that Molly hadn't given it up. And she listened to his voice, a voice like a river, both flowing over her and holding her up. A voice she had known like the back of her hand. Known it as it usually was—controlled and full of authority, the voice of an editor, of a director, of someone who knew what he wanted—and its vulnerable underside as he reached out his hand to touch her cheek, asking if she might be interested, if she didn't feel it, too, this thing between them, this tug at the center of being. And she had. Of course she had. She'd never spoken so easily with anyone, unless it was Leo when she first met him, and yet she'd held back, held him at bay, trying to think what her life was, what it would be like. And then she'd stopped singing and stopped talking to Ted on the phone and stopped most of her life and slowly he had faded. And here he was, sounding as young as he'd ever been, and she felt older, so much older, so that she felt a qualm, after all, and needed to buoy herself up to reply that yes, she had meant it, and she'd be there. On Thursday. It would be so good to see him. It had been too long.

Her voice, more mature, slightly distant, but of course they wouldn't have the same easy intimacy after all this time. Still, it had been good to hear her. To know she was coming out of her shell. She seemed as though she was emerging from something—a cocoon—something that had held her until she was ready. And now she was ready. Her voice. Nothing changes in a voice, not until age has really set in. How would she look? Thinner, perhaps. Or heavier. You can't tell that from a voice. And her hair, maybe with blond streaks. Long or short? Women do so many things with their hair. He should have asked about Leo, but now it was too late, the phone back in its cradle and he couldn't call back, appear too eager, and besides, there was no knowing what she'd be like. He'd have to wait for Thursday, and even then, with things so busy, it would be hard to tell. Have to take things slowly, but things had always been slow between them. Slow and steady and inevitable, as it had seemed to him. But death has a way of cutting out the inevitable. Or making it imperative. Thursday. Tomorrow. It was hard to wait.

That'll be Leo, she thought when the phone rang again. But it was Jackie, across the street. Her water had broken, three weeks early, and Bob was on his way. He'd have to come in from the city and then take her back to the city to State Methodist Hospital, and she was worried. It all seemed to be happening too quickly. Could Molly watch the boys until one when Mrs. Westworth from next door would watch them until her teenage daughter, Sheri, came home from school? Could Molly take over for the rest of the morning, she wouldn't ask like this, but it was an emergency. And, of course, Molly could take over. She didn't have anything else to do. A baby, on her anniversary. Maybe she'd tell Jackie that it was her anniversary, to give the baby a welcome. She'd watch out the window and as soon as Bob arrived, she'd be right over. Or maybe sooner, because Jackie probably wasn't packed or ready. Not that you had to pack much for the hospital these days because they let you out so soon. She would come home tired to demanding three- and four-year-olds, how could she do that, except that she was so young, resilient, more resilient than Molly remembered ever being. But then Molly'd been old for a first-time mother, almost forty, and something of a sensation at the hospital because it had, in the end, been so very easy. As though her body were built for birth. And she'd wondered why she hadn't had dozens of babies, hundreds of babies, all from this body that seemed to know exactly what to do. Not that she'd liked the feeling of being out of control, her mind not in control, her body going ahead doing what it needed to do without so much as a say-so from her mind. She'd hated that, the animal in her. Did men ever find themselves reduced to animals? Maybe sex, she supposed, but even then there was some control, not just hormones set in motion and the body rolling with the punches, pushing and pushing new life into the world. Screams. She'd heard screams from a room down the hall, or was it next door, but who was screaming? Who was resisting and screaming her individual self to the world? She'd been so good, really, gripping the bars on the bed and holding back her sounds, her mother would have said she was ladylike even in these circumstances, but really, she would have screamed if she'd needed to, but just when it felt as though her whole body was a wave of pain, as though she would surely need something to take it all away or she couldn't go on, they'd said let's go and wheeled her into the delivery room and then her mind was back with her and she could watch in the mirror and everything seemed so fascinating that she almost forgot to push and they yelled at her and she pushed and then there he was, even then his hair sticking straight up and wailing so they called him "porcupine." And then he was quiet and looking around, dazed, and she was dazed, too, because he was there before she had had to struggle and she almost wished there had been more pain so she could own him more deeply.

But you didn't own children, she knew that. You loved them and raised them but they had a self, she'd seen that even then as he looked around, puzzled, and she'd sensed it later as he became that personality she recognized as Arjay. Such a stupid name, really, not a name at all. She'd wanted Daniel, because it was both Irish and Jewish. She'd wanted Danny, and if they'd called him Danny maybe he'd still be here, another little boy with another self. But Leo had wanted a boy so badly, wanted to start over and do it all right, and wanted to name him after his grandfather who had just died at the age of ninety-eight. And so he became Arjay, her Arjay with his strange little face and his silly hair. Strange, when she had visited the grave, she hadn't recognized him there on the tiny stone: Rudolph Joseph Bluhm, 1987–1991, beloved. That wasn't Arjay. That was another little boy, with a strange name lying here with all the ancient relatives, surrounded by old people who died when they were meant to die. She hated the graveyard. She'd never be in it, next to him, because she didn't belong, wouldn't be allowed, she suspected. She'd always wanted cremation. Ashes, clean and simple and reduced to the elements. Ashes in the bay in Maine, even if it meant doing something illegal to dump them overboard. She wanted to rock and float and then sink into the depths of the place she loved. She wanted to be buffeted by storms, and to be insulated from them. She wanted all her fire in the sunset over the bay.

Only in winter. She'd gone once in winter to where the gravestones rose above the snow. Everything white and completed. Everything smooth and shapeless and somehow peaceful, and she'd felt that Arjay would have liked it there under the blue sky with a few flakes falling and the world sucking in its breath it was so quiet and dignified. And then she hadn't gone back again because that image was enough, the strange name that marked her loss and that seemed, after all, no part of her as it settled into the false brightness of the scene.

But now she needed to get ready for two lively living boys who would be excited and confused and all the things children feel when their mother is swept away from them by the tides of adult concern. She'd bring the quilt, that would be a nice surprise. And she could make it easier by telling them exactly what would happen and when their mother would be coming home and all those things that parents forgot to tell because they were so caught up in the responsibility of keeping things going. She'd be useful. So when she dialed Leo, it was to tell him what was going on and why she'd be across the road and not at home when he tried to call her. But he was teaching and there was no answer and the phone rolled over to the secretary who also seemed to be out and so it rolled over again to the voice mail that Leo might or might not check when he got back from teaching. There was nothing to do but leave the message, which lost its edge by being told into a machine instead of a living ear. She knew people who could talk into the machines as though to the person and those messages sounded so sincere and animated, but she always went stiff and formal, aware that this was not meant to quicken the brain or light the eyes, but simply to give information. "Listen, Leo, I'll be across the road at Jackie's for a while watching her boys. She's going into labor and Bob is taking her to the hospital. You might try calling there later this afternoon to see how she's doing—it's so close to your office, you might stop

in if she's had the baby. Call me if you get the chance."
Maybe she should have said something about dinner,
but really, she wanted him to remember. It wasn't a
test so much as a desire, an urgent desire that he remember her on this date. At least this one.

And then Bob was turning into the drive and she
was hurrying across the road and Jackie was walking
to the car and Andy and Jacob were waving with her
as the car backed out and seemed to rush back toward
where it had come from. Five minutes, not more than
five minutes, and they were gone. These two little
boys were about to have a brother or sister, weren't
they lucky, and did they know their father would
come home to watch them tonight and that Sheri
would watch them this afternoon but first they'd all
think about lunch and what did they like for lunch,
she'd bet peanut butter, or macaroni, how would they
like some macaroni, and maybe they could show her
their toys and they'd find a game to play until Sheri's
mother came over while they took their nap.

Jackie, looking back for a moment, saw her two
boys waving and hoped that Molly would manage.
She'd never really seen her with children, only known
her as a friendly neighbor who kept mostly to herself.
Seen her red car drive off early in the morning and
return by midafternoon. Wondered what she did, because she didn't seem to keep regular hours. Someone had told her that she used to teach chorus at the
high school, a part-time job, but that she'd given that
up when her son was born. But now she seemed to
have some sort of job. Consultant, someone said. But

consultant covered too much territory, and she didn't know what Molly could consult about. But she was friendly and she'd tooted when she left this morning and so she'd come instantly to mind when she needed someone. What was this baby doing coming so early when she'd arranged for Sheri to help because it would be summer vacation and now this was the last week of school and Sheri would not be available all the time, what with graduation and everything else that high-school students attend. But they would manage. Still, Lynne was turning out to be inconvenient right from the start. Maybe she'd make up for it by being an easy delivery. By the third time around, something should get easier.

Bob had been surprised by the call, too. This was not a good day to have a baby. He was in the middle of a project at work that could not wait. And now it seemed that it would have to wait. But his boss wouldn't be happy about this, which put a kind of pressure on him, as if the baby weren't pressure enough. He'd wanted the baby and Jackie hadn't quite wanted it and she hadn't seemed to warm up to the idea the way he thought she would when she was closer to the event. He didn't even know why he wanted three, given how expensive college education was definitely going to be by the time they were that age, and given the way his own family had turned out. There were three of them and they hardly ever talked to one another, lived scattered all over the country and called on Christmas or Thanksgiving and traded having their parents for the holidays, but didn't get together much themselves. Of course, his brother had three of his own, which didn't make it easy. And his sister had decided not to have any at all, which made her impossible when the kids acted up. His mother hardly noticed. He'd told her Jackie was pregnant and she'd said "that's nice, dear" in her usual voice and he wondered whether she'd really heard what he said. And his father had said "why?" in such a blunt manner that Bob himself had wondered why and that was the end of that conversation. As soon as he got Jackie settled, he'd call and make sure the boys were being good and talk to them a bit. They'd hardly had time to tell them he'd be coming home. They must be confused and frightened and he wondered if Molly would understand. Strange woman. She seemed always to be waiting for something, that look people have when they are waiting, partly there and partly already in the future. But it was nice of her to come.

Molly wondered what had happened to blocks. And drawing paper. Those had seemed to her the best toys to have. Now everything was plastic. Everything moved or made noise or beeped. Everything did something, but there was nothing for the boys to do. Nothing to build or draw, though they did have crayons and coloring books. But that's not the same; the picture is there for you. So she found an old sheaf of computer paper and unscrolled it on the kitchen table and called out questions as she began cooking. "Who can draw me a picture of a family?" "Who can make a mountain and a sun?" "Who can make a funny-colored ocean?" "What do you think the new baby will look like?" Anything to let them go inside, to where anything is possible. Because shouldn't childhood give you at least that? A sense of possibility. And she laughed at the purple ocean with its orange fish in a blue bathing suit. And she laughed as she stirred the pasta and grated the cheese. Molly, the woman from across the street who waved at them and dressed up like a witch on Halloween and sometimes asked them questions about their action figures, was laughing and it was the first time they'd ever really seen her laugh. They drew another bathing suit.

The phone rang while they were eating lunch at the picnic table because they'd decided to leave the drawings of the baby and the bathing suits for their mother as a surprise when she came home, so Molly told Bob she couldn't talk because the boys were outside, but how were things and that it's a good day to have a baby—her anniversary—and how was Jackie and that was good and did he want to talk to Andy? Jacob was already droopy eyed over his macaroni and she thought she'd try to tuck him in bed. In the background she heard Andy tell him about the bathing suits and wished he'd kept them as a surprise because it sounded sort of silly over the phone, we put bathing suits on all the fish, when Bob probably had so much more on his mind, but Jacob nestled into her shoulder as she lifted him up and she knew she had at least one ready for a nap. Strange to have a little body so close to her own. The way they seemed to fit into all the curves, nature so clever with all of it, and clever, too, she guessed, at the way they grow out of those curves and into the envelope of their bodies. Tucked away safely inside the self where thoughts could be private and peculiar even as the world thought them normal. These two boys would play Little League baseball, or maybe soccer, she hoped soccer, such a beautiful, fluid game, all the children spilling over the field with so much energy in October light, not like the singular, stilted positions of baseball, especially with children who couldn't really make those seamless plays that stitched the game together. She hoped soccer with the slant light giving everything a glow and the ball like magic between their feet and their shouts distinct and clear, like a spoon on crystal, over the distances of the afternoon. So when he hung up, she played for a while with Andy, kicking the ball back and forth and making a game of not being able to touch it until he, too, looked tired and she suggested he'd need to rest quietly and wait for Sheri's mother. And that was that. The house quiet, but not empty, dishes to wash. If she got home in time, she'd make a casserole for them all and have it ready. Not the ginger pasta because the boys wouldn't like that, but something simple. Not the salmon either, for the same reason, but she probably had something they would like tucked away in the cupboards and she'd try to leave something. Though they could always order pizza, would probably rather order pizza, a little excitement showing up at their door. Maybe she'd call ahead and pay for pizza and leave Bob a note that all he had to do was call in his order. That's what she'd do. Too bad, though, because the thought of baking and puttering in her kitchen was appealing. Though it was so hot, maybe this was the best idea. Yes, maybe she shouldn't get too involved. Wonder whether it will be a boy or a girl. Such a moment of suspense. It was so important, somehow, hovering on the brink of knowledge, waiting for that knowledge to settle into fact, a boy, you have a baby boy, a healthy, bright, baby boy. And then she had cried. Leo had his boy. She'd had a baby, she'd done something she hadn't planned to do, had given up the dream of doing, and it was done, done, here he was, with his solemn gaze and silky hair. Fuzzy, all lit up by the sun, like a halo really, though she hadn't thought that then, just a haze of hair, like soft down, to nuzzle and kiss and mumble and be silly about.

Though she wasn't silly. Practical, really. Sensible. She'd been sensible. So this was memory intensified to romanticism and she didn't really like that in herself. She much preferred the woman who knew what had happened to her. If only Leo could have loved her enough, could have touched her and cried with her and made aching love to her so that together they could have recovered. If only Leo hadn't pulled himself back into himself, nursing his wounds by loving her in ways she didn't want to be loved. She could remember when she first saw him through the crowd at the bar after she'd finished singing the Irish songs that were the feature of the evening, his dignity, the grey hair at his temples, his sweater just informal enough, but his manner formal, almost stiff, yet enthusiastic, animated, as he hurried up to ask her about the origins of one of the songs, something he thought he could trace to a Yiddish tune he'd heard from his grandmother. And they were alike, those songs, though when he sang it, it was not the same tune, more joyous than hers, even though sometimes it went into a minor key while hers stayed poised on the tip of the major key, ready to slide into sadness but rising above it.

DAMN, HE'D TRIED CALLING once before going to class and the line had been busy. And then he'd had to teach and after that he'd agreed to meet Steve for lunch and he had a tennis date with Harvey, so there would be no time till late afternoon. Too bad, because he knew he'd rushed out this morning and she didn't really like that, liked to talk through what the day was going to bring. Part of that was because his schedule changed so often, certainly semester by semester, and now in the summer it was different yet again, and the time for dinner changed, time for breakfast, everything needed to alter to fit his new class schedule. And there were meetings and lectures and all those things she needed to be informed about, had the right to be informed about, though he kept forgetting to tell her and then when she was unhappy he got angry and the cycle began. He wasn't not thinking of her, not really, but he didn't really actively think of her the way she thought of him. He knew that. Knew that he let his life carry him away, take over, dictate his timing. It was a way of being alive in the moment, not having to think of the future. And not having to think of the past, which he rarely did, just plugged away at the task at hand. And right now that was teaching a class in literature to students who, for the most part, weren't interested but needed another three credits in order to fill one requirement or another. They wouldn't have read the book or be prepared to talk and he'd be left trying to pull it out of them, wring it out of them the way his mother had wrung the water out of their clothes as she washed them out in the kitchen sink. Not even a washing machine for his early years. Just the sink, and clothes drying on lines in the kitchen, and his mother worrying when he spilled because it meant another shirt to wash before he'd worn it twice. These students wouldn't know about things like that, wouldn't believe it, even. They thought it was old hat that somebody had walked on the moon, thought that the old days were *Leave It To Beaver,* talked about the books as though all their ideas were alien. They couldn't "relate." They liked it best when he let them get into groups to discuss the books and they could complain to each other about how hard the vocabulary was and how it didn't make any sense and reinforce each other's complaints. They thought that was a good class and often said so at the end, "Great class, Doc," they said, when he'd done nothing, given them nothing of his sense of how the book spoke to all of history. Great class, as long as you don't give us one of your lectures and don't force us to think in ways we don't want to think.

Except for Steve, who was the shining light this summer. Just by accident, Leo had him in his class. Because he lived in Columbus, but went to another college, in Philadelphia. Here he was, though, taking his course and reading his books and writing papers that were electric with their questions and their speculations. Alive. So at lunch he'd talk to him about his plans for the future, plant the seed, ever so carefully, about graduate school. Casually mention one or two he thought were pretty good, some professors who weren't so caught up in theory they didn't have time for the text itself. Because Steve was old-fashioned, a real reader, connecting what he read for Leo with what he'd done in physics or learned in philosophy. Putting knowledge together like a puzzle rather than trying to dissect his life into tiny one-hour fragments. Acting as though he wanted to learn, not as though he wanted to spout an already formed opinion. A breath of fresh air. And so likable, in a challenging sort of way. Came from a Catholic family, but was putting that behind him. The perfect student. What he'd dreamed of for thirty years. And to have him come like this, out of the blue, for a summer, a godsend. Someone to think about and plan for and lecture to. Someone to pass something down to, like a legacy, his love of Joyce and Faulkner and now Graham Swift. Someone to show that it wasn't in vain, all those writers working away with nothing but the future in mind. The vague and mysterious future with its potholes and quicksands and silent traps to keep you from emerging at the other side unscathed. Because who came through living unscathed? That's what he learned every time he opened the pages of a book. That he wasn't alone.

Who had she been talking to? He often wondered that when he got the busy signal. Her private life was so very private, if he asked later she might say "no one" or genuinely not seem to be able to recall any conversations. Could be credit-card companies, trying for the few housewives left at home. Or possibly thinking that now so many people had found a way to work out of their homes that they were perfect prey. Or a friend, though her friends had thinned a bit, called less frequently. Or work. Sometimes he forgot that she worked, too, though at tax time when she brought the records he could see that she had contributed quite a lot to their income. But her work was, if anything, more sporadic than his. Yet it never interfered, took place only during school hours. Evaluations of student musical ability, in six separate counties. She was often called to recommend a course of study. To connect talented students with musicians in the city, that sort of thing. Sometimes she talked about a particular student and his ears perked up. He liked it when she seemed involved. Liked the way her voice rose so intensely and circled around her ideas until she forced them into a cohesive whole. Her mind was so different from his, and

yet that was what had attracted him, after that first
night when it was simply her voice meeting his
loneliness head-on. He imagined the headlines of
their lives.

## SHORT BUT TO THE POINT

There once was a woman who wanted a man to call.
She wanted him to want to call. There is no other
way to say that. She wanted him to want.

## SAD

It wasn't the right word for what either of them were
feeling. She was, in fact, the exact opposite of sad.
And that does not mean she was happy. It means she
was alert to her own possibilities, she was aware that
the sun was shining and that the grass was green. She
was willing to walk out into the day and see what it
would bring. She was not sad, because sad meant she
wanted only her own four walls and her own under-
standing company. Today she was not sad, but its opposite. He was, in fact, not sad, but not exactly its
opposite. He was lost in that drift to somewhere else.
This does not mean he was alert to his own possibilities. He was, however, alert to the possibilities of
others. Steve, for instance, who might survive him.
Would certainly survive him, and therefore should
have the benefit of his goodwill.

She had the steady clack of railroad trains, teacups from her mother's set, and songs. He had the Friday-night candles. She had farmland, the seasons, the names of all the birds and flowers. He had one day when his father had taken him fishing. She had her fat-wheeled bicycle in the photo album upstairs. He had his favorite aunt dancing in the kitchen to the sound of big bands. She had her first marriage. He had his first marriage. He had sense. She had sensibility.

## LIFE ON THE RAW

Neither of them knew what that meant. They had each been coddled and comforted. Had been reared in the cradle of family. Oh, they'd had their poverties, but not their impoverishments. They'd had trials and tribulations, but small trials and ordinary tribulations. They'd had grief, and that was raw. But not life on the raw. Because even their grief had been modestly middle-class and insulated.

## ERIN, GREEN GEM OF THE SILVER SEA

It was so derivative, Professor Bluhm thought. So much like photographs of itself. The green was like nothing he had seen. And the sea was silver, at least sometimes, or pewter. Yes, pewter, dulled to perfection. Those great cliffs, and people lying on their stomachs, looking over. The week after they went, someone fell off. Dashed to the rocks, he supposed. In a pewter sea. The green was like April. Stenciled green, the fields so tiny they looked like stamps, tiny green stamps to affix to an envelope. If you had to name a gem, it would be an emerald. And that, too, felt derivative.

## SUFFICIENT FOR THE DAY . . .

was the evil thereof. But there had been no evil that they could see. Only blue sky. Unto. Untoward. The day had yielded, so far in its young existence: one yellow quilt, one audition to be performed on the next day, one neat drawing on a roll of computer paper, one class taught, one lunch almost finished, one long, unending memory, one baby about to be born.

## AND IT WAS THE FEAST OF THE PASSOVER

All the plagues. They love the plagues. Who would have imagined? It was hard to know what to do, and when to do it. Everyone talking at once. Drinking wine, then arguing that you weren't supposed to drink it yet. A drone of Hebrew that Leo surprised her by knowing. She supposed he had memories of his grandfather, his tiny figure raising his glass, but she had none of those memories to keep her sitting there, in the midst of the confusion, waiting for the plagues to catch her attention.

## SHINDY IN WELLKNOWN RESTAURANT

Not so well known, the student union, but convenient. Not a shindy, exactly, but still. A lunch in which Professor Bluhm suggests, somewhat diffidently, that prize student, Steve, consider following in his footsteps. A lunch in which Steve, quite politely, wonders aloud if that would make sense. There is, after all, the Internet. And you could really make money in computers. And his buddy, Buck, was already making twenty grand part-time while he was going to school. Hacking against the hackers. It was the latest thing. A lunch in which the latest thing was healthy choice, chicken-salad sandwich on wheat, with cranberry juice. A lunch in which the latest thing was one of the women in the class, he didn't know her name, the dark-haired one who sat in back. A lunch in which he wondered if it made sense to make the old man so happy just by knowing Beckett. He should take a cue from Beckett and be quiet.

## CLEVER, VERY

Couldn't help it. Had to play out his theories. Had to make puns and play around because where else would he have an audience like this one? Sang Emily Dickinson to the tune of "Yellow Rose of Texas," sang Robert Frost to the tune of "Hernando's Hideaway." This was not news. Not news that stayed news. Where had Leo been all his life? He called him Leo now, though tomorrow he'd say Professor Bluhm in the class. Where had he been, that he'd laugh that hard at the obvious? He and Buck knew all those songs. You could sing Frost to "O Tannenbaum," too. The woods grew more solemn that way, but the horse was still funny.

## FROM THE FATHERS

All those memories. Separate memories joined together in holy matrimony. Her father with his head in his hands. His father with his hands on his head. Her father with his blue Irish eyes. His father with his extreme myopia. Her father with his burst of tune. His father with his litany of wrongs. His father with his angers and his hurts. His father with his columns of numbers and his terrified wrists. His father who could drown her father in the volume of his need.

## DEAR DIRTY DUBLIN

Dr. Bluhm had preferred it, though he hadn't dared say so. She'd been enchanted by the west, its blackberry brambles and winding lanes. She'd felt as though she had grown up there, the landscape that familiar. It stepped right out of the songs, she'd said. But he'd liked the dirt and the streaming crowds of Europeans and the hot, cramped pubs with their scent of Guinness. He'd liked the way the wind threw grit in your face and you sometimes had to walk backward down the alleys. He'd liked the dark buildings that were, just then, being sandblasted to restore the original color. Too bad, he'd thought, they'll erase the very charm, which is the charm of darkness and history and the dear long list of the dead.

## INTERVIEW WITH THE EDITOR

That would be Ted. There was no one to ask the questions, so he asked himself. Will you be happy to see her again? Yes. What will you say? Yes. Will she be happy to see you again? Yes. What will she say? Yes. Are you still interested? Yes. How do you know? Yes. Where will you go? Yes. Does this make sense to you? Yes. Is there anything to which you might answer no? Yes.

## EXIT BLOOM

Né Bluhm. For his tennis game. He exits left, Steve exits right. They agree to meet later that day, at the bookstore café, where they can resume their conversation. Steve secretly resolves not to be so glib. Leo secretly resolves to back away from graduate school. Steve secretly thinks that Leo looks a bit like his father. Leo secretly thinks that Steve is handsome, with his shiny black eyes. They couldn't be black, but dark, as though they swallowed light. He didn't usually think that way—that's why he'd noticed. He turned left and hurried toward the locker room. He did not look back. He did not pass Go. He did not collect $200.

## EXIT BLOOM

Leo doesn't notice the lack of flowers. He does not know the names of flowers. He doesn't say daffodil, he says yellow flower. He doesn't know the daffodils have come and gone, that all he sees now, in early summer, is dandelion. If he were to see them on the strip between the sidewalk and the road, he would say to himself, look at all those little yellow flowers. But he does not see them. He is lost in thought.

## RHYMES AND REASONS

There were no reasons. They all knew that. Ted couldn't say why Molly's voice made him go soft in the belly. Leo couldn't say why he could look so hard at everyone but himself. Molly couldn't say why she was suddenly ready. Bob couldn't say why he wanted this child. Jackie couldn't say why she didn't feel ready. Lucy couldn't say why she had suddenly, out of the blue, asked Molly the question. Marcie couldn't say why she couldn't say why. Harvey couldn't say simply because he couldn't say. Steve couldn't say because he didn't know. Brian could say, but he didn't choose to. There were no reasons, only rhymes. Headline, head-on, neon. Boyle, spoil. Bluhm, come. Lynne, wean. Andy, handy, Jacob, hiccup, Jackie, lucky, Bob, job, Brian, fryin', Steve, leave, Harvey, larvae, Lucy, juicy, Molly, falling, Leo, see O, hearsay, no, nothing rhymes with Arjay.

### KYRIE ELEISON!

Like bells. The voices sounded like bells. Short, sharp bells in crystal air. Rising on air. Like fireflies. A flicker. The church alive with bells. The voice of the bells. Soprano. Filtered through the tissue of the air. Not joy, exactly, but certainly not sad. Brilliant, they sounded yellow in clear air. They sounded like glass.

### ???

There were enough questions left over for everyone. None of them knew exactly how to phrase them. They hovered over their heads like a tiny swarm of gnats. Those little flies that cluster in June air and make it impossible. They hovered over their heads as though you could swat them away with answers. But there were too many, and they were too small. Their fingers raked the air and still the questions hovered.

HE ORDINARY VOICES OF ORDI-
nary children, giving her back her
unexceptional life. That's what she was thinking as
she left Jackie's, leaving the boys with Sheri's mother
and telling her about the paid-for pizza. "How
thoughtful," she'd said, but it wasn't really thoughtful. Expedient is more like it, but when better to be
expedient than when you had no idea when a baby
would be born. That's one thing about them—they
come in their own sweet time and, for the first and
nearly the only time, the world revolves around
them. The other time is death, which also comes unbidden, though sometimes as foreseen as a parturi-
tion. But those boys were alive, energetic, full of what
they had yet to become. And Jacob's little body
against her shoulder had felt fine. She'd enjoyed the
feeling. Her body felt renewed, as though she had
stepped out into a wintry day and returned with
bright cheeks and a healthy appetite.

Would Leo have called? There ought to be something on the answering machine. But when she went in to check, the red light kept its steady tone, no blink at all, though her eyes willed it to blink. Nothing. No one. And it was after one, so he'd finished teaching and now where would he be? She followed him in her imagination, through the halls of the university, back into his office where he might—or might not—have received her own message, then out across the campus to lunch at the union, then where? He always found something else to do so he didn't come home in the middle of the afternoon, though it was summer and he could do that with ease if he wanted. So probably tennis. Leo loved tennis. With his friend Harvey. She'd never seen what he saw in him, so fastidious and, well, fatuous. She didn't like tennis, the game so circumscribed, the lines so straight and predictable. Back and forth, back and forth, oh, she knew there had to be nuance, but it eluded her, or rather, didn't capture her imagination, not like other games—soccer, and even baseball—with their spark, their moments of brilliance. But he seemed to like the way he could count on his body, could push it to act in a preordained pattern. They were different, really, in what they wanted, of each other, of the world, of their own bodies. She wanted to feel what she'd felt when the songs belonged to the air alone, before they were captured in print and reduced to a court and a net and a set of rules. She wanted her body to flow out into the air and follow the sound over the hills, the way she'd done when she was a child lying in bed listening to the low moan of the diesel's horn at the crossing, letting it carry her beyond the valley and into the future where its funnel of light probed the darkness.

No message, so she still didn't know what they'd be doing tonight. And if Leo did go to see Jackie, he'd be later than usual. Maybe she could meet him there, but the two of them would be too many. Maybe she could meet him at a restaurant after all, even if it did mean two cars coming back, their half-lives following each other home over the familiar route.

Expressway to arterial to two-lane to busy intersection to village streets and then on out onto their own curving road where houses had sprouted almost overnight where there once was a farm that had seemed to give the space a purpose. We are nothing in this world, she was thinking, and yet we have such heavy feet, such a way of marking it off, setting the stakes, and staking the claim. We are nothing, our lives so ephemeral, lost in the long pull of history. Less than a song, which seems to have a life of its own, passed down from generation to generation so that what is remembered is the song, not the singer.

It was the same with love, she guessed, equally ephemeral. How many times had she loved, she wondered? Were they all love? They all seemed somehow so different, and yet she'd named them each love. How different they'd been, though, depending on her own volume of knowledge. The boys in school and college, of course, that's the way she'd learned to love. Learned to listen to the body, the way it seemed to want to show itself off. The breasts in tight sweaters. Skirts, fluid on the legs. Fluid, and waiting. Wanted roughness. And sometimes solace. The way a touch could make her go hollow and aching, an ache that seemed as though it could never be filled. And then Joe, who she'd married, and that had been love in its own solemn way. And the one brief affair she'd had in Savannah—that was love, too, unexpected and intense and meant for its four-day duration. Ted, she supposed, or almost Ted. She'd been on the brink. And Leo, always Leo, the one she'd left everything for. The one who made her wait.

Waited first while he worked through the aftermath of divorce, always disappearing to meet some woman in Michigan, then reappearing, picking up the phone as though nothing had intervened. Then, more galling still, the woman in the city where Molly would sometimes come across his car parked in front of her real estate business, the two of them probably off in a café somewhere not far away, but his car big as life parked on Park Avenue right when she was on her way back from school. A slap in the face. His car, with his license plates, no mistaking it, until her stomach turned. So when he'd call again she would beg him to stop, to let her recover and go on with her life. But the phone would ring and she would answer and it would begin all over, the expectant hope, the imagined pressure of his fingers on her cheek, the imagined voice in her ear saying low, sweet things, singing maybe, something from his past. It would begin all over, her heart like a buoy for the lobster boats she'd seen all her life, bobbing along the surface but tethered to the bottom of the sea, tethered to her desire that did not see itself in the mirror of his eyes, but why? why?

She was still waiting, clearly, waiting for him to call, waiting for him to remember. As though she were knitting and then unraveling the stitches, watching time stand still, marking its stasis. But out in the yard, the flowers did not wait; they came up no matter what happened—even late frost, or a windstorm tearing away the petals of the tulips. It was late, now, and the spring flowers had almost faded, leaving the borders to leaf and shadow. But the daylilies were coming early, and she'd pick some now for a centerpiece. Leo liked orange. A spot of color to pull the room together, like little tongues bellowing their presence, big band flashing its trumpets. It would remind her of Matisse, she knew, orange flowers in a purple vase, set out on the dark blue cloth. She dared to do that, dared to let the colors find themselves and bleed into her life like a watercolor, blurring the boundaries between branch and horizon, everything part of everything else. The spark of it all. She was waiting for something to sound like those flowers on her table.

When the phone rang again—like a summons she thought—then that must be Leo, but how could it be since he'd more than likely still be at lunch? It was Marcie. Her voice like sandpaper. The sulky center of it all. "Where's my dad? I can't get him at his office." As though Molly could produce him on cue, as though she hadn't had her own trouble getting him at his office, as though he had called her to let her know where he was and what he was doing. "I haven't been able to reach him myself." How judicious she sounded, and on purpose, since her instinct was to say something else, something like, "Thank you for asking, I'm fine, dear." Something like, "Have you ever thought of me as anything but someone to order around." Something like . . . but her mind would not supply a snappy response and if she indulged herself she'd find a thousand grudges to mull over the entire afternoon. Nothing was settled between them, nothing finished. Molly wasn't sure what was needed, but something more than the status quo. "I've changed my plans, so I won't be here after six. Have him call me before that. I really need to talk to him."

She wouldn't serve that function, she decided. What if he didn't call? He often didn't return Marcie's calls, even when she gave him the message, even when she explained what she perceived as Marcie's urgency. It would be her fault. It would be her getting between them, even when she had done nothing except exist, the person who answered the phone, the person who conveyed the message. So this time she asserted herself. "No, I don't know when I'll see him. You call back here and I won't pick it up; then you can leave the message for him. And leave another on his phone at work. I'm just on my way out."

No asking where she was going, just the click and then the steady ringing again and again while Molly waited, counted the five rings before the machine would begin its litany, waited, listening, while Marcie was leaving her father her message, which sounded just as peremptory when she was speaking to him as it had when she'd talked to her, so maybe it was simply her unfortunate manner, not personal, not aimed at the woman who had married her father. Just aimed at the world in general, as though the world owed her attention. Maybe all she needed was to know that he thought of her, but he'd have to let her know that. Molly had done what she could, and now when she thought of Marcie she thought of the way her stomach knotted at the sound of her voice; thought of the way she had accused them of being cheap when they wanted to use the over-Saturday plane fares, not a midweek fling; thought of that awful moment when she wouldn't stand up at their wedding so that the judge stopped the whole cere-mony and asked her to please stand up. It flooded over her in spite of her resolve to keep it at bay.

And she blamed Leo, knew she blamed Leo, first for not protecting her from it, for not saying he couldn't—wouldn't—see her treated that way, and then for being so afraid that he'd let his own child manipulate him. She didn't want to see that as a weakness, because she needed his strength, needed him to make her days endurable, needed to think of him thinking of her. Which was why she wanted the phone to ring and make everything translucent.

But it didn't ring. Sat there stoic and silent, a constant reminder in its very silence, like someone not speaking, so that you're doubly aware of their presence. She hated the way she waited. Remembered, so often, the days she waited inside her small apartment, wondering when the phone would ring. Would he call? Would he remember to call? And Leo, meanwhile, living his life, classes and coffee and papers to grade and people to meet and readings and lectures and occasionally Molly to call, or Molly to invite for coffee, if he could find the time. She'd always known when he was going to leave for Michigan; about two weeks before, he'd stop ordering beer for lunch, or would refuse the pie in his favorite coffee shop. And then she'd know. Because for someone else he always seemed to want to lose a few pounds, look his best, while with Molly, he ordered the beer, didn't seem to mind the extra pound or two. And it had made her heart sink, knowing he would be going and knowing he wouldn't tell her until the day before, then toss it off, as though it meant nothing, hadn't he told her he'd be away, back on Sunday, and then he'd call. As casual as paper blowing in the wind. As unconcerned.

And then when he was gone she still couldn't leave, not because she was waiting but because she was devastated. Paced the room, then sat at her desk, trying to work on a project, a collection of old tunes and their variations. She could go to work, but when she returned, it was as though she had shut off her feelings, living on cold sandwiches and coffee, living for the news to come on so she could turn off the lights and drift off to where she wasn't pacing like a panther in a zoo, wasn't so filled with restless energy that she didn't know how to hold herself together.

She had waited herself into a state; she knew that. And she wasn't going to let that happen again, not even on the small scale it had become—the lost evening or the late lunch, the thirty minutes in the car while he returned a video at the supermarket. And it wasn't the same, she knew that, but so reminiscent that her old self surfaced in those moments, frightened and insecure. No one would know it to look at her, she made sure of that, but she knew that other self was there, just offstage, waiting to take her over. Leo knew, too, though he pretended he didn't. He was good at pretending, and that made her cautious. Sometimes she watched him pretend and felt herself fade. Almost colorless in the version of her life that she couldn't recognize, no matter how hard she tried. Drowning, that's what she felt at those moments. Sucked underwater, unable to breathe, panic-stricken, a flailing of arms and legs and nothing to breathe, knowing there was nothing to breathe.

Her father with his head between his hands. All the other men, exhausted and defeated, their heads bowed in defeat. That's what she remembered about the flood. Or, no, there was more. Her father hoisting her onto his back in the dark of midnight, walking through waist-deep water down the road toward the Erwins' farm. Brian on her mother's back. The water swirling and angry, reflecting nothing in the rainy night. Darker than the air around it. Noisy. And then she was sitting on the polished hardwood floor of the Erwins' farmhouse while the women carried furniture up the stairs. The men were in the barns. The children were drinking orange juice when she'd seen it, water creeping through the grate of the hot-air register. Water spilling out onto the floor.

From upstairs, they heard them, the men pushing open the huge front doors and walking knee-deep through the downstairs. And then, even at five, she could tell their voices were different, subdued, suffused with despair. She saw them sitting on the steps, their heads in their hands, and it took a minute to figure out which one was her father. She listened, but they said nothing. Sat with their heads in their hands. It was her mother who told her they hadn't been able to save the cows. Hadn't been able to push their heads underwater so they could clear the stanchions that trapped them there in their orderly rows. They'd wrestled and pushed at the panicky cattle and only a few had let them push them under in order to let them swim free. The rest were doomed. And the men, each in his separate memory, tried to drown out the frightened mooing, the flailing legs and the stubborn, ignorant resistance to their arms. Stupid cows. Too stupid to be saved. Stupid flood. Stupid to live so close to a river. Stupid to think that they were immune.

In the morning, a rowboat came through the front doors right to the stairway where, from the fifth step, they were handed into the boat and taken to higher land. The water had a sheen, almost calm, as it spread itself over the landscape, oblivious to the river and its current. She could see her house in the distance, rising out of the water like an ark. And when they came back two days later, her mother spent an hour crying, then set to work, scouring the fine silt that had settled in the teacups in the cupboards, washing the curtains and bedspreads, throwing away soggy carpet, warped drawers.

That was not drowning, she knew, but fighting back. Her mother knew how to survive. Yet Molly had felt as though she were drowning, as though the water had risen and she had nothing left to do but stand in her stall and let it complete its mission. She'd felt that way about loving Leo, and then again about losing Arjay, and now she looked up. From the kitchen window she could see an old apple tree, its new green leaves caught in a tangle of sky so blue it seemed to rise in a vault. Air in safekeeping. She would not drown on a day like today.

HE TEAKETTLE'S WHISTLE. LIKE a train, only more impatient. Trains were not so restless, knowing they were already on the move. Knowing that the sound floated out behind them, demarcation of where they had been, not where they were going. Already nostalgic for the next hill, the next town. Tea. That's what she wanted. A cup of hot tea, even if the day was warm. Not from a microwave—that made it taste different. Tea was a comfort, and after that she'd think of how to fill the afternoon. She'd set the table in the dining room, just in case, those slate blue place mats on the dark blue cloth, then all six turquoise candles, maybe the cut-glass water glasses she'd found at the thrift shop, and those purple-grey plates from Maine, dusky, the color of sunset on the ocean. And pale green salad bowls, almost the color of the endive. She needed tomatoes, but how to find good ones? And if she spent the afternoon on tomatoes, she'd be committing herself to this dinner she didn't want to make, this event she

didn't want to have to create, and what if he'd forgotten so deeply that he had nothing for her? He could make up for that with a dinner, but there would be no pretending if she cooked the dinner and his stricken look revealed what she suspected, which was that he didn't have a clue that today was June 16th. Just a Wednesday at the end of the century, middle of the week when he'd taught for two days and still had two more to go. Wednesday, as plain and ordinary a day as you could pick. It hadn't been a Wednesday when they were married. Odd the way dates revolve in this way. She'd been born on a Wednesday, before dawn, when babies are usually born. Wednesday's child is full of woe—she'd hated that. She'd been a happy child, really, contemplative, lost in her books, but also singing, climbing trees, riding her bicycle down tree-lined streets. The woe would come later, but she hadn't known that. Had seen herself as discontent, but essentially happy. A happy discontent, if there could be such a thing, and she was living proof that there could. It was just that she always wanted something more, like those trains at the crossing, wanted to be going and seeing and taking in the world.

When had she become content to sit in her home? Or to spend her time in Maine staring out to sea, watching the lobstermen make their rounds, watching the waves roll in and in and in with such precision? How had she become the placid woman she felt herself to be? Or, if not placid, then bereft of the old passions, as though she had folded them neatly in tissue paper and packed them away. If she pulled them out again they would smell faintly of cedar and would look unfamiliar, a part of her past. But fifty wasn't old, isn't old, can be the beginning of things as well as the end. The big Five-0 they'd shouted on her last birthday and she'd laughed and done a little dance. Still, the words had been devastating. Not that she minded having reached that age and admitting it, not that she was thinking she'd lived well over half her life, though clearly she had, but that she wondered how it added up, everything she'd done and everything she hadn't had the chance to do.

Leo still had a chance with Marcie, but he didn't seem to know how to do it. He'd always looked up surprised when she'd told Arjay to behave, as though you couldn't really expect a child to behave. Behave, she'd said, shape up, or I'll make you sit on the couch. And Arjay had settled down as often as not, and soon he'd be running his little trucks through the tunnel he'd built of blocks, humming to himself, or talking, "Here comes greenie, right behind you, bluey," his voice happy again, happy to be in control of himself and happy that his mother wanted him happy, not whiny or kicking or whatever had made her say *behave* in the first place. It had come so naturally that it was hard to imagine someone not knowing you could have that sure authority. Not that he hadn't had his tantrums, but she'd handled them as though they would get him nowhere but a quiet few minutes on the couch and then on with his day. Not that he could command and she would obey. She had wanted her own time to think her own thoughts, had hoarded her time alone. Sometimes she felt guilty about that, but it's a good thing you don't anticipate death because it's best to think you have all the time in the world, then the small things you do will not feel so significant. So she forgave herself those stolen moments when she'd say play by yourself, find something to do, because they were good for a child, any child, even one who wasn't going to live as long as you expected.

Maybe there were still some blocks in the attic. She'd give them to Andy and Jacob. It was so hard to imagine a house without blocks. A computer and a plastic pretend computer, but no blocks. No way for the mind to build a shape it will then inhabit. No place to escape to, to play by yourself in. She remembered going to the phone company and getting Arjay an old used phone so he could hold conversations with his stuffed animals. Now the play phones talked to you, said the same things over and over, no surprise, no, "Okay yellow bear I'll see you next week when you come back from the forest." And then at night, "Yellow bear's gone to the forest so I'm sleeping with tiger until he gets back." And then in the morning, finding yellow bear in the den, surrounded by branches blown off the apple tree, a veritable forest, with a little box as his suitcase and inside the box, a stone and a scrap of red paper and no way to know what that meant.

Molly, taking her tea out to sit by the apple tree, looked up to the patches of sky above and thought how blue, not subtle like the ocean, but a clear, inno-cent blue—the blue of October, but it's June, so it holds out more promise, while in October it's the poignant holdout blue of things in decline. This blue was almost excruciating with its sense of things un-folding. The leaves intensified it. Not like blossoms, which carry their own color and make the sky go pale. These leaves would deepen until they approached a burnished copper and the scant apples that appeared would be hard to see, hidden in camouflage. It never looked as though there was much fruit, and then a windy day would spill them on the ground like mar-bles and she'd wish she had picked them, wish she had known they were there, waiting for her.

She and Brian used to climb the apple tree in their backyard, inching out onto the fattest limbs and working their way toward the tips so the branch would dip and sway, suddenly unstable. Their father shouted the day the limb cracked and set them on the ground, shouted that they were stupid, how many times had he told them (and he had), but the branch had always held, so solid, until this time they'd ex-ceeded its limits.

Brian, hot and hurried, coming back to work from a late lunch near the Capitol, glanced up at the cherry trees, just turning into their summer look. The red-dish bark almost glowed in the afternoon sun. He and Molly had preferred the apple trees, larger and more inventive, offering nooks and crannies where they could hide in the leaves and watch the activi-ties below them—mostly their father puttering in the garden, weeding, or transplanting, picking up stones. The yard had been a creek bed at some time or other, so many stones, so many he called them his best harvest. Some time lost in history because the river was blocks away from this new house. Not after the last flood, their mother had said. She wanted something foolproof. Funny, he thought, the way I sometimes think of Molly and feel she must have been thinking of me. As though there were connections over hundreds of miles and weeks of silence. Not that they weren't friendly, quite the contrary, but that they didn't talk all that often, didn't see each other all that much. God, she was brave, he didn't think he'd have been able to face it. And she had, he knew that, even though others thought she had simply retreated behind a wall. No, that wasn't like her. She'd looked it in the face and then taken it into herself, emerging a couple of years later with a sense of what life would—and wouldn't—let her have. On her fiftieth birthday, she'd told him that she wanted him to be the one to tell the doctors to stop the machines, if it came to that. Leo won't be able to, she'd said, and I know you will know what I want. Just like that, and he'd said yes, of course, because, of course, he did know what she'd want. But that she was thinking in this way. . . . Not morbid, not really, but wondering who, when she didn't have a child to make the inevitable decision. The way he'd had to make it for their father. Turn it off, he'd said, but the doctors thought it was too soon. Molly crying on the phone that it was inhuman, that he didn't want to be what he'd be if they found a way to make him live. And Brian knowing she was right, insistent, and the doctors looking uncomfortable, not looking him in the face, as though his insistence were obscene, when it was humane, when it was what his father had asked him to do so many times he felt no qualms, nothing like a hint of doubt. She hadn't been there, then, because it was just too soon after Arjay. She would be of no use, she'd said, and she'd known herself. He liked the way she knew herself, wished he knew himself half as well.

No one would think he didn't know himself, assertive and entertaining, the mask hardened into a way of being. But deep down he counted on her to make him face the truths he might otherwise avoid. Oh god, her anniversary, and he hadn't sent a card. Hadn't remembered until just this minute and now he was due back in the office, no time to find a card, and besides, it would obviously come late. A phone call would be better. Lucky they hadn't gone to Maine this month, where it was always hard to reach them. Someone would be home, or at least the answering machine, and maybe he'd wire flowers. Yes, Molly would like that, the drama of the truck arriving, the little card with its message. She liked to think someone was thinking of her; and she always made you feel as though she'd been thinking of you, postcards, little gifts that seemed just right, as though she'd been listening hard to your inner thoughts. He still used the golf balls from Ireland, could always find his ball because it was different, was from the place where their grandfather had grown up, or great-grandfather, Molly would know, and what was that place called? She'd called from there, wanting to put him in touch with his past, but it wasn't really his past, was it, just the origins of his past, the poverty and ignorance that drove them off the farm and across an ocean. A romanticized past, once it had suffered its sea change, so that every Irish bar in America celebrated as heroic what was merely necessity. Green on St. Patrick's Day, when what had the church done for any of them but keep them in ignorance? Thank god his father had thrown that off, too, or he'd have had a harder time telling the doctors.

She has a memory like a rock, he was thinking, as he looked up the florist's number in the yellow pages. She remembered everything, every little detail. How did she do that? Just a couple of weeks ago she'd asked, do you remember the flood? What made her think of that, he wondered. No, he didn't remember. Only the stories they told afterward. Didn't remember the night swelling around them, the water at their waists. Didn't remember the clear, smooth wood of the floor as water spilled across it. Always she told it the same exact way, the orange juice and the hot-air register. It had gotten to where he could almost see it, that vivid an image, but if he were honest, he didn't remember, though he had a vague flicker of sitting in a high chair. He'd been three and she was five, so there was a reason, though she remembered being three as well, remembered the day they brought him home. Seemed to remember back to the crib. The paint tasted dusty, she'd told him, and their mother had confirmed that she had chewed the paint off the top bar, standing there waiting for someone to get her.

Iris, he said, definitively, snatching it out from the names of the flowers the woman was reading. Iris would please her. 7 Larch Lane. Hard to think of it as Larch Lane when it had been Eccles Road where he'd turn up occasionally, always glad at that final turn out of Dublin proper, the city behind him and then the village and now only the three miles of swollen countryside before he'd arrive at their long driveway. 7 Larch Lane, before 4:00 this afternoon. Credit-card number. So easy to do something on short notice. Probably could have done it himself over the Internet. Showed his age that he didn't think of that first.

Odd that her anniversary was only three days after the date of their father's death, though she couldn't have planned that out beforehand. If only he'd died before Arjay, hadn't had to watch her grieving and then die before he could see her recovered. So many broken lives, interrupted before there was closure. Almost made you want there to be an afterlife, just so you could catch up on what you'd missed. Odd idea, really. Their father's ashes still in a box in the basement. He'd been waiting until Molly was ready to scatter them, somewhere near Sinking Spring, but they'd never quite got around to deciding, and now it seemed somehow like a lost opportunity, something past its time. Still, maybe they could go back, dump his ashes over the fence near the apple tree, no one would notice, and then he'd be home where he'd spent so many of his evenings digging and planting. Probably a law against such things. Probably a law against scattering them over a creek, or the lake, so what were they going to do? Didn't really want to think of someone finding them after he himself was dead. What's in this box? That sort of thing. He'd have to talk to Molly about it. She'd call to thank him tomorrow and he'd bring it up.

In the side yard, Molly was thinking about Brian. She was thinking about their father and the way he had shouted when the branch broke, setting them roughly down on the earth. His shout extended into the future, so that now she could feel herself falling. And she could peel the memory back until she was eight again, stretched out on a limb close to breaking. And she can peel that memory back until something sets it all in motion: Molly and Brian climb the apple tree—the one their father held together with a chain when lightning split its forked trunk. Willed it into living. They edge their way out on the large limbs to where they begin to creak and sway. The bark underneath their fingers is old and smooth, worn smooth by their climbing, their slippery weight. They hide there in the camouflage, watching as their father bends to pull the weeds near the new stalks of corn, stands up to wipe the sweat from his forehead, bends again. Watch as he balances the stones vertically along the top of his stone wall, fitting each in place as though it will be there a century later. Watch as he splits the cherry logs with his long-handled ax. Can almost smell their fragrance when, next winter, they will fill the rooms with this moment when, small below them, he still seems larger than life.

THREE HOURS OF AN AFTERNOON stretching like canvas. If she were in Maine, she'd go out on the deck with a book and be happy. Every once in a while she'd look up, notice the slight differences in the horizon, a boat with a sail, or a wisp of fine cloud, the changing colors as sun glinted on waves. The sounds, too, always changing. Wind in the scrub pines. Waves coming in and in again, steady as time itself. Or else she would wander down the road to where the wild blueberries grew— but that would be later in the season—letting the sun beat on her back until it softened and expanded. She'd pick the berries in a fever of sunlight. Tiny globes of flavor, the juice staining her fingers purple. She'd bake a pie using single-malt scotch instead of water as her liquid, and let it bubble in the oven, the crust heaving up and down like a lung. There would be no trouble finding something to do if she were in Maine, where her songs got lost on the wind and she never felt self-conscious singing into the height of the day. But here she could not sing. Felt foolish singing, even if she sat at the piano and pretended she was seriously practicing. Not even in the shower. She didn't like showers, preferred baths. Not the long luxurious baths of the women's magazines (who ever had time for candles and bubbles and deep, dark towels?) but simply the practical bath of a woman who liked a moment to relax and wanted to soak the bottoms of her feet. Dove soap and shampoo and a plain cotton washcloth.

Those are the things you should know about someone. Washcloth or sponge. Dove or Crabtree & Evelyn's Savannah Gardens. That would mean intimacy. Savannah, she hadn't meant anything when she was thinking about soap, but there it was again, city of flowers. Or it had been when she was there that March, left in a snowstorm, returned in a snowstorm, but four days of azaleas, hiatus, her whole life on hold. All those pretty central squares a festival of color, and the houses, drawing you to them as if they could take you inside, take you into a past of cotillions and carriage rides and dinners served on fine china. A time she didn't even believe in, but briefly coveted.

When he asked her to dance that night, it wasn't as though he were a stranger. She'd known Neil, on and off, for several years. Glad to see him there at the conference, a familiar face, a coincidence actually, seeing him there in the South instead of at the local conference where everything would have been different. Of course she'd sit with him at the dinner, someone to talk to while they were politely meeting others as well, talking shop, because at least he'd know where she'd come from, who she was when she wasn't who she was right then. And so when he asked her to dance it was natural, wasn't it? But his body had been so comfortable, as though hers were meant to fit it, the way his hand folded hers into his chest and they didn't need to look at each other or make small talk because they each had come out of a snowstorm and now they found themselves far from home.

Sometimes she wondered where he was now, what he was doing. He'd moved to California, she knew that much. That had been before Leo, but it had been the beginning of Leo because it had been the beginning of the ending with Joe. What a long slow process, the body readying itself for its ravages. The quickened pulse that told her Leo was coming long before they had met. The body going soft, dazed at the core, and desire sprouting like a crocus overnight at the touch of a hand folding hers to his chest. Until she was burning with it, frantic, more needy than she'd ever been, and she was the one who was rushing them into her room, into her bed.

That was flying, she thought, flying off into a vast sky. Not drowning, which was deceptive, the sluggish water, calm on the surface, static, not a sign of all those cows under its glassy veneer.

It was what the water left that was terrifying. Not only all the bodies, still slumped in their stanchions, but the slimy residue that seemed to bind all their belongings together. Mud at the center, the earth making itself known. And the huge tree deposited in their front yard—ripped from its place somewhere miles upstream and left on their doorstep. She remembered her uncles and her father calling themselves the Downriver Construction Company. The way they sang and laughed and stopped to drink a beer or two while they sawed and sawed, hand saws, long two-handled crosscut saws, weekend after weekend until the tree was a pile of logs by the chicken coop. *And it's no nay never, no nay never no more will I play the wild rover no nay never no more.* And the way they fixed the tangled plumbing and built new cabinets to replace the ones they ripped out. Down to the studs, the house exposed, with the smell of wet plaster and always the stale scent of silt, as though something wild had been set loose in the house.

Only 1:30. Time had gone so quickly when she was with Andy and Jacob and then seemed to halt. Stopped to let memory take over, and today she didn't want to remember, but to act. She'd drive into the city, meet Leo around five, to hell with waiting for him to call. She'd tell him what they were going to do. And before that she'd stop to see Ted, take the bull by the horns, see him before the awkwardness of the audition made her diffident. See him and let him see her. Then they wouldn't have to be ill at ease in front of the others. Had to be done today because tomorrow was Thursday. She hadn't been thinking about that this morning, how close it was, but there was no turning back. At any rate, she didn't want to turn back.

If only. Time to stop the if onlys. Leo wasn't going to turn to her now, pull her to him, draw her hand to his chest. He wasn't going to pinch her bottom or laugh or tug at her ear or move sensuously against her in the dead of the night. He wasn't going to touch her into fire, her nipples erect and her body alert. Because it hadn't happened for years now and no, it wasn't going to happen again tonight even if it was their anniversary, even if it had started that way, so intense she couldn't bear it, or couldn't bear the way her body burned when his was so nonchalant.

This time, when she called, the secretary was there. No, she hadn't seen Leo since early this morning. Yes, she'd leave a note in his box. He usually came in partway through the afternoon, caught up on business, talked to the chairman, that sort of thing. She'd leave a note on his door as well, just in case. Because, she was thinking, these professors never know what they're doing, say nothing of when. They'd forget everything in an instant of idea. She'd seen them stand by the copier wondering what they'd come for, turn and walk away, leaving the letter in the machine to be fished out by her and left in their mailboxes. She'd seen them begin a conversation and then veer, suddenly, into another, as though thought could travel that fast, could change gears that quickly, and she guessed it could, because they seemed to follow each other's ideas well enough to argue, well enough to make puns and play around with ideas as though they were real, as though you could reach out and touch them. But she didn't say that to Molly because

Molly was a wife and she always told the wives that she'd leave a message and she always did and some-times they called them back, and sometimes they didn't.

And Leo, on his way from lunch with Steve to his tennis date with Harvey, stopped in the campus bookstore, still reeling with the ideas he'd bandied about with Steve over chicken sandwiches at the union. That young man had a head on his shoulders, no doubt about that, jibing at him about Beckett, about wasn't he the flip side of Joyce, the alter ego? Most people, Steve had proclaimed, have a flip side to *themselves,* like Woody Allen in *Zelig* and *Broad-way Danny Rose.* Shakespeare, too, making fun of his own tragedies when he sicced comedy on them. But Beckett had a flip side to someone else. His mind like a sword, no, not a sword, but those long pointed things they use in fencing—rapiers, that was it. Like a rapier, a thrust and a jab.

The bookstore was reasonable, for a campus. The usual mugs and sweatshirts, but also aisles of real books, something other than textbooks. And a fairly good coffee house. On one table, a new book by Edna O'Brien. He'd never read her, but Molly did, he knew. Sometimes she read out passages and they were al-ways fine, though somehow so disturbingly female. Fetid. Or damp. Still, he should buy it for her. She was the one who had forced him to read Graham Swift and now look, he was one of his favorites, someone he taught whenever he could. Molly was more active a reader, really, than he was, and yet he didn't give her enough credit. Bought her best-sellers when her taste was really more subtle. Didn't remember which books she owned, so bought her the ones he knew he hadn't seen around the house. But this was a new book, signed, because the author had come to campus a month ago. He should have told her, but it had slipped his mind until she'd come and gone. But a signed copy . . . that would make her happy. And he opened the book briefly, read a few paragraphs in the middle of a story, felt himself sucked into the female whiff of emotion, and snapped it shut. $21.95. A lot to pay for a book these days, but still, a signed copy . . .

What should she wear? She should dress up for the restaurant, but then she'd be too dressed for an informal chat with Ted. Maybe they could eat somewhere less formal, somewhere funky, or trendy. Somewhere fun. If she took Leo to the pub where they'd met—mostly fried food—it wouldn't be the meal that mattered, but the reason for the meal. Yes, that would kill both birds with the stone of her intention. She could be casual, casually there. For one, because she didn't want it to seem as though it was anything but a last-minute idea. For another, because he might have forgotten, and so she didn't want to make too big a deal over it. And if he called before she left, then she could change her mind again. It wasn't as though it was carved in stone.

Odd to have thought about Joe today. In all divorces, there's a leaver and a leavee. And the leavee gets the sympathy, inherits the friends, at least when there was no good reason to be left. The leaver has another kind of grief, and no one wants to hear how hard it is to leave, how the mind whirls through a thousand reasons not to leave while the body wills itself to go. No one wants to hear how it haunts you, years later, that you'd had to steel yourself to keep on walking. That you'd had to turn your back on someone who had never turned his back on you.

In the past fifteen years, she'd found one or two others who understood. Leavers themselves. Leavers who had never been abused, or abandoned. Who understood what it was to drown in a life of your own choosing. But they were few and far between. This was simply not an area where she could find instant empathy. Odd to think of Joe without guilt, or the pang of recrimination. She ought to call him, maybe next week, see how he's doing. You can't live with someone for thirteen years without caring how they are doing. Caring that they are in the world, that the world is going on with their presence in it. Suddenly she couldn't bear the thought of a world without Joe. Without Leo or Ted or all the other men she had loved in one way or another. A world bereft.

They all had three letters in their names. What did that say about her? Joe, Leo, Ted—and Neil, four letters, but one syllable. Not like Sebastian or Nathaniel or even Martin or Howard or Roger, one of those names that can't be shortened easily without sounding silly. Short, quick names, like an exhalation. A whisper. The names had come out of her mouth and made a shape in the air. An imprint.

And she'd followed the trail to see where it would take her.

But it had taken her here, to an afternoon with little to do, and more at stake than she cared to think of. Junction of past and present, so that Leo's failure to call now was his failure to call then. He never believed her when she told him the past flooded over her, became the present, but here it was again, the current with its awful force, making her think what she hadn't wanted to think of.

Walking toward the men's locker room, Leo thought of thighs. Students in shorts. Or skirts too short to be called a skirt. Smooth thighs, settling themselves into the curvature of the desks. The one older woman who crossed and recrossed her legs so that he didn't know where to look he was so busy looking away. Thighs carefully hidden in jeans, though a good pair of jeans was what he liked best, the way they strained a bit at the seams and you could almost feel your hands on the backsides. A friendly slap. Fanny. Butt. Cheeks. Rear. Bottom. Tush. Derrière. It was the same old story, the same old restlessness. The penis twitching, half hard in your own jeans. Meant to keep you on your toes, on the balls of your feet, get you in the balls. Meant to stir you up, stand you up, strike while the iron is hot. Meant to make you hot, bothered, both heard. God, he hadn't been fair to Molly when they first met, going off then coming back, like a yo-yo, hurting her more deeply every time. But he wasn't ready. Just after the divorce, with all that messiness still inside him, yet her voice had made him calm. Reminded him of his grandmother, he couldn't quite tell why. Maybe it was the tune. Yes, probably the tune, because his grandmother had had a deeper voice, but when she hummed it went to a higher register, as though sorrow belonged on another scale. Or happiness. It was hard to tell which, they seemed so intertwined.

Jeans, blouse, sandals, socks, scarf, flimsy scarf. Short, sharp names for what she was laying out on the bed, testing for their degree of informality. Maybe linen slacks instead. Then, if they decided . . . yes, linen slacks and the scarf, to dress it up or down. She'd put some earrings in her purse. No socks. She'd just look as though she were too hot for stockings. Olive green with pale blue, and the scarf a gauze of purples and greens. Yes. And her navy sandals. The ones she bought last year in Maine. And in her mouth, one of her uncle's songs:

> *When I was single I wore a plaid shawl*
> *But now that I'm married I'll wear none at all*
> *Still I love him, I'll forgive him*
> *I'll go with him wherever he goes.*

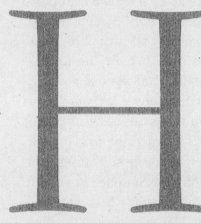ARVEY WAS LATE, SO
Leo watched the coeds
on the next court—one blond, one what they'd always called dirty blond—their sturdy legs as they
stretched for the serve, or ran for a volley. Already
tan, so early in the season. But then, sometimes their
legs were tan in December, tanning parlors dotting
the blocks near the university. "10-Minute Speed
Bed" or "52 Bulb Cyberdome," the signs read, though
just what that meant he wasn't sure. And no one
wore white anymore, so they played in neon shorts,
their hair pulled back in ponytails. Still, as he
watched, there was the old tug of desire, a flutter in
his stomach as their bodies seemed to float across the
surface of the court. Their laughter, voices bright
as butter, high and uncomplicated. They had their
whole lives to live ahead of them, and here they were,
middle of June 1999, thinking only of the evening,
of young men and pizza and beer and the latest
music, thinking nothing of Bosnia or Iraq or the next

millennium. Medicine was advancing by leaps and bounds, but still he doubted they'd see the next hundred years. They didn't realize how monumental it was to be alive when the clocks all turned to 2000. He'd always known he'd probably see the millennium turn; born in the 1940s it had seemed possible, but distant, something to think about later, and now later was upon him. Two thousand years of what? Every autumn, when he celebrated the Jewish New Year, he tried to remember the count, something over five thousand, but what? 5038? Sounded good, but probably was far off. Why couldn't he remember, when it was his new year? Never paid enough attention, though he always meant to. Meant to take it more seriously. It was only fate of birth that his parents were not killed in the Holocaust. He knew that. But his life had seemed so ordinary, so reliable. It wasn't that his imagination failed him, because he'd had nightmares, god knows, in which babies were flung aside and mothers sent to the gas chambers, nightmares more real than any dream, and of course he'd seen dozens of photos, movies, shrunken bodies that, he knew, were his, his skeleton beneath the skin, his skull beneath the wiry hair. He was not immune, never immune, but it seemed so far away. Faded in the bright sunlight surrounding the tennis court on a university in the middle of America. Faded in the face of young women's bodies, supple and fluent, and the ball back and forth, back and forth, with its little thunk against the racquet, its new trajectory.

They had noticed him watching, he could tell, and

they had changed their game subtly, taking him into account. Women weren't supposed to do that any more, but they did. They shifted their bodies slightly, let the breasts show, looked his direction then looked quickly away. Flirting. But not admitting they were flirting. How would he look to them? Old? He didn't feel old. He was in good shape, body well tuned, trim from jogging and these near-daily games of tennis or squash. Hair gone grey at the sides, but it had been that way for fifteen years, since the time of the divorce. So he hadn't aged that much, had he? Just more sophisticated. Not the skinny kid in high school who played tennis because he couldn't play football. And then Harvey was there and they were taking out their racquets and warming up and he was aware of the women watching him, aware of his muscles, the way his lean body looked dancing slightly on his toes awaiting one of Harvey's usually ill-disguised drop shots. Felt himself twisting and turning and leaping, like a fish out of water, like those salmon they'd seen climbing the ladders at the locks in Seattle. Leaping, so filled with the urge to live, and those blonds, their bright eyes watching even as they played their own game, now slowed a little, so they could keep track of two things at once.

And then he forgot them. He needed to beat Harvey this afternoon. Yesterday, he'd been slack, forgetful, a bit lost in reverie, and Harvey had surprised him by taking advantage. The games had mounted almost in spite of him, 15-love, 30-love, 30-15, 40-15, game. Just like that. But today he felt fresh and ready, fresh from his lunch with Steve, his mind sparked by challenge, and now this physical challenge to keep him alert. And the women watching. He didn't want them to see him lose his edge. Deuce, ad, deuce, ad Leo, game.

This time she got his voice mail. "Leo Bluhm is not in his office at the moment. Please leave your name, number, and when you can be reached." Well, he knew her name, her number, and when she could be reached, and he hadn't been calling, had he? Lunch and then tennis—it wasn't as though she didn't know what he did—but that they had needed to communicate about the day, their day, the one they shared, or would share. It would be different if he had a simple nine-to-five job, if he returned home at the same time each evening, if they sat down to a regular dinner and watched television and went to bed. Then she would know he had simply forgotten what day it was and she would take things into her own hands. Or she thought she would, at least that is what she imagined she would do if she were in different circumstances. Their life was constant surprise, or at least constant mutability. He could turn in the drive right then, or he could come back late, after a normal dinner hour, having met with a student who could only come at six, something like that. And she needed to know. She wanted something with a sure connection, something like those old-fashioned systems they used to have in department stores where the clerk put the sales slip and your money in a little canister that whizzed up through the ceiling to an invisible room where someone looked everything over, sent back the change, the canister zooming back to where it came from, like magic. She and Brian had loved to go to Gordimer's with their mother just to watch them all floating through space, making a universe of their own, whizzing back and forth filled with dollars and quarters, those days before credit cards, really even before checks were common. And it was fast—faster than now when it seemed that everybody made you wait while they typed in so much information that it would be easier to come armed with a hundred-dollar bill. But they'd look at you strangely, then think it might be counterfeit, and you'd still have to wait while they approved the acceptance of money, real money.

That's what she'd liked about Ireland, the feeling that a punt was a punt and it still had some power. The way the men would put some money down on the bar and suddenly a round of pints would appear in front of the fiddlers, the man with the flute or accordion. The way the postmistress would count out the change first, then take some back for the biscuits you'd told her to add to the stamps. The way life had slowed down to the pace of walking, to the sound of the ponies on the pavement on the way up to the Gap of Dunloe. To birdcall and blackberry and cloud sifting over the sun. She'd wanted to go find the town where her grandfather had been born, just another American looking for a past, but she'd found the past in the life itself. Not in the graveyard, which, she'd had to admit, made her want for the first time to be buried, to be somewhere so sheltered and communal, to be within earshot of the sea with its pewter winds and its shushing spray. But the life was there in the eyes of the people who seemed to have time to listen to each other. The stories they told. The long walk back from the pub at the top of the hill, picking their way by flashlight down the road, a stray dog barking once in a while and the moon a backdrop to the paper-cutout mountains. Others ahead of them, and yet others behind. A scrap of song. And laughter. So much laughter.

In the morning, she'd look out at the little town with its pastel houses strung out along the coast and she'd wonder why anyone would leave this place, what hardships there must have been to make someone pack up and turn his back and never look around. It was not romanticism, but the real question that must have occurred to Irishman after Irishman, and the women, too, when they'd worked hard all day and then walked out onto the bare streets of Boston in the evening. So the long memory had begun, the homeland, a place of warm fires and cups of tea and large families. Not a place of poverty, drunken rages, too little food for too many faces. And the memory reached back and back, found its place in all the myths, then tugged at the knot that held them all in its spell. She'd felt it when her uncle Terry sang, *But come ye back when summer's in the meadow. . .* letting his tenor rise over the ocean until it landed in Dingle, the sea change that broke out in a broken key, almost a wail of longing.

They'd only spent three weeks, but it was the two in the west of Ireland that she carried with her. The sight of the lake at dusk, or the mountains struggling out of the mist. Not Dublin, with its busy streets, its heat, its computer-crazy youth with their bleached hair and nose rings, its interchangeable addresses. Might as well be Prague, she'd thought, or Cincinnati. Except for St. Stephen's Green, which seemed to move back into the last century. Old men feeding pigeons and small boys in short pants sailing boats in the pond. Young women stretched out on the grass for their lunch hour. A buzz of voices, rarefied, drifting from the past. She'd thought she heard the voice of her great-grandmother, Marion Tweedy, or someone like her, there in St. Stephen's Green.

Leo had loved it, loved the pubs and the way people talked so freely to strangers and the music. Had soaked up everything, reading six newspapers a day. He was the one who learned about "begrudgement"—the kind of envy that snatches defeat from the jaws of victory. A mental outlook, nothing could be as good as it might seem. He felt right at home in it as a Jew, he'd said, laughing. Felt right at home with thousands of years of oppression at his back. Wouldn't have felt as comfortable in Prague. Or, god forbid, Russia. Not even Israel with its traffic and its fast pace and its computers. But here, here was where literature began, in the stories people told, and why they told them. Began in the place where memory holds sway. "I love Ireland," he'd shouted, and the people in the pub had cheered and bought him another pint.

In the middle of Lough Leane, that island: monastery, ancient tumbled stone, yew tree misshapenly shaping itself to the wall. On one branch: a magpie, disheveled after a night on the town. How easily he moved across water—flight and return, flight and return. Music driven from within, not completely wholesome, as though something were missing and needed to be filled. Irish charm, red-haired and rumpled. But at the heart of it all something stubbornly imprecise. She couldn't define it, but she felt it inside her, like a bloodline, though she didn't believe you could inherit a culture you didn't live within. Still, the stories trailed after them, into the new land, made their way into her bedtimes, the Downriver Construction Company singing "The Rose of Tralee" as they fitted the pipes.

What was the blood she brought to this marriage? Her father's heritage so strong, and her mother's so much weaker. German. Odd irony that she was half German and Leo would maybe never have looked at her if it had been the other way around, if her father's name had been Schmidt, and so her own. O'Rourke wasn't a threat, but Schmidt, even though its translation made it so clearly lower class, carried with it the threat of annihilation. Still, her mother's family had been here for so many years, since the early 1800s when they came as indentured servants, transplanted from the cities of Europe to the farms of North America, ending up in small German-speaking enclaves, Springerle for Christmas, sausage, not much else in the way of tradition. And certainly not the longing for the homeland, the looking back. No, they'd looked so continuously forward that they'd moved west, then farther west, settling in Ohio. Farmers, from a bunch of tailor's apprentices. From the city's underclass. But such bright farms, sturdy and dependable, the regular rows of corn and the cows tight in their sheds. Sturdy peasant farms filled with sturdy peasant women, yet something had happened to make them ashamed of their names. The war, Hitler, yes, of course. But they were Americans by then, had been for a hundred years, or more, and still the power of the old country to claim them, even when their sons went to fight like her mother's brother, Uncle Edward. To claim a bloodline, as though her mother contained the root source of evil. Her mother, with her deep blue eyes and her practical shoes. Her rolling pin with designs of thistles, pinecones, hummingbirds, imprinted on the dough, and under that, the anise taste of caraway, an undertaste of forest and deep-throated fear.

But the songs her family sang were Irish tunes. And they dreamed, always, of finding their way back to County Kerry. Back to the green-black hills, shorn of trees, and the wind worrying away at the chimney. On St. Patrick's Day, they all wore green and ate corned beef and potatoes and cabbage and drank green beer and wished themselves back to a life that none of them had ever lived. Still, Molly thought of herself as Irish, and it always surprised her to realize she was really half and half.

So when they had planned the trip, two summers after Arjay's death, something to take themselves out of themselves, it was Ireland she'd hankered for, as though the land itself could heal her. And in many ways it had. Had brought her to life again, though maybe no one could tell, watching her stare out to sea, looking toward America where she had been born. The sea reeked of darkness. She couldn't bear its unbearable burden. Time to undo what time had done.

Life, gone underground, like a silent river. They'd come home and found the place in Maine, the place where she could stare eastward, into the same headstrong sea. Sometimes she stood for half an hour, without moving, simply conjuring up the Celtic crosses in the little graveyard at Beaufort, her family name fading in the corrosive salt air, stone becoming stone, though, come to think of it, the ogham stones in the farmer's field nearby held the traces of an untranslatable language, proof positive that something carved in stone can stand the test of time.

How had Leo had that plot all planned for? He must have made the arrangements during those three months of agony, waiting for the doctors to find the cure that they could see would not be coming. In the face of her fierce denial, he must have turned one day, picked up the phone, and made plans to put him with his people. Funny, she denied, then accepted. He'd done the opposite. They were ships passing in the night. There must have been a moment when they occupied the same territory, but if so, neither one had been able to recognize it. If she'd known, what would she have done? Cried, screamed probably. Fought it tooth and nail. How could he put him where she could never be with him? Never. And if she'd seen Beaufort before that, would that have given her comfort? A sense of continuity? Though now, today, the day to remember the ceremony that had created him in the first place, there was hardly continuity. Voice mail. Missed messages. Unspoken plans. And Marcie's insistent demands, to tug him out of this life and into something else, something vaguely threatening, like the family plot, all the old names: Virag. How had it become Bluhm for some of them, remained intact for others? Ellis Island, some clerk or other, the V like a B, and the rest indecipherable. A name assigned, as though you could shuck off the past just like that. Thirteen, his grandfather had been, and maybe you could. What does thirteen know of the past? It only looks forward. Looks around, and up and down, but not backward. Wants a new stereo and Nikes and mountain bikes. Wants to play soccer and not have to go to Maine with its parents. Wants its privacy, e-mail, pizza and Coke. Or nose rings like the young men in Dublin. Tattoos. The trappings of difference, to hide how much it is like everyone else. How much we all are like everyone else. So few emotions to go around. The endless variations. The formlessness of it all.

He has such good form, Harvey was thinking, as

Leo began his last serve. In tennis, in writing, in the way he lives his life. He is nothing if not form. A villanelle, Harvey thought, not as tightly knit as a sonnet, but complex. Its recurring patterns, deepening, turning toward a foreseeable end. Yes, a villanelle. Maybe he'd tell Leo that, in the shower. They'd laugh. Seeing each other in literary terms. But his body, too, was a villanelle, shaped and shapely. Those girls on the next court noticed it, he could tell. Not girls, really, but it was hard to call women so young anything else. In his father's day, they would have been girls. Maybe not so much because of their age, because women had married younger, he knew, but because of the giggling, the absolute freedom of their voices, the bodies that he'd bet anything were virgin. Virgin territory. Not a mark on them. Not a young man with his probing fingers or an older one with his knowing erection. Nothing. Nada. They were altogether too intact.

He'd ask Leo in the shower what he thought. Whether or not . . . no, they had ponytails, for chrissakes. And one was chewing bubblegum.

T HE SUN WAS PAST ITS HIGHEST point, the garden beginning to take on the shadows of afternoon. They'd grow longer, blue-grey, inching across the yard until they reached the side porch where, late on a summer day, she could find a cool spot, a bit of a breeze. Not an ocean breeze, but one that carried with it the faint scent of things growing, must have drifted from the south where farms still spread out their fields. The corn now a few inches high. Some rain on into July and there would be no problems.

If she didn't hurry, there would be no time to see Ted before she'd have to meet Leo. It would be better to leave plenty of time. If it didn't go well, she could stop in the bookstore or something, waiting for Leo, but if it did go well, she didn't want to have to keep looking at her watch, showing her anxiety. Voice mail again. Where was he? He should be back from tennis by now. "Listen, Leo, I've been thinking we ought to celebrate. I'll come into town to meet you.

Your office, at five-thirty. If you get a chance, check in on Jackie before that, will you? I'll take you to the pub." What more could she do? She'd covered all the bases. And she'd leave a note here at home, just in case he was already on his way, and then they'd . . . she needed to call him back and leave an alternative plan. "Listen, Leo, me again. If you happen to come home, oh, well, I'll leave something in a note for you because, of course, if you come home you won't get this message at all." Stupid, she should have thought that out beforehand. So now the note:

> I've gone to pick you up at your office to take you out to celebrate. If you happened to come home instead of back to your office, then I'll call you sometime after five-thirty (when I planned to meet you) and we can make plans from there.

That should do it. She wished they could have talked. She'd have felt better, but now she needed to hurry. As she backed down the driveway, she looked up at the house, so familiar, and yet suddenly strange, too, too large for the two of them, too perfected. Too much a part of the suburb it now found itself in, too perfectly painted and trimmed and landscaped, when what it wanted to be was an easygoing farmhouse. She'd had the horrible asbestos shingles removed the first year they were there, and then the careful restoration of the wood and the professional painters. White with black shutters, and a new set of triple-glazed windows. Then they'd glassed in the back porch to make a sunroom, and after that there was the patio, laid out in a crisscross of ycllow bricks. The sun was still too high, but sometimes when she backed out, it hit the windows at such an angle that they stared back with sightless eyes. Blank and indecipherable. At those times, the house scared her, its masks, the hidden life behind the windows that wasn't much of a life these days. She felt like going back to draw the curtains, to protect the privacy of the house itself.

Because it knew what happened inside its carefully plastered walls, its wallpaper and hardwood floors and restored ceilings. It knew the way they circled each other so carefully, so polite and refined, so considerate. And it wanted them to scream at each other, to throw things and dent the plaster and make gashes and stains. It wanted them to peel away their mutual solicitation and call out to the other from a selfish core of need. Me. Me. Look at me. It held their secrets and kept them well, and when she was inside its protective walls, she felt safe. But now, pulling away, she felt as though while she was gone, the house would rise up against her.

She'd felt that way sometimes when Marcie spent the summers there, as though the house itself was an enemy. Her stomach would sink when she turned in the drive, knowing that whatever she had bought at the supermarket, Marcie would claim she hated—the food, the brand, the size—nothing was right for her. And her voice would stick in Molly's head. She couldn't seem to forgive its adolescent arrogance, its "duhs" and "come off its" and the way her mouth turned up in a condescending little smile. She'd try to convince herself that there was no ill will, just teenage self-centeredness, but then something would come out of the blue to convince her otherwise. The deliberate quality of her remarks: "Is *she* coming, too, Dad?" She's in the way; we don't want her; why do I have to be here with her; I will never accept her, all rolled into one snippy tone, one pointed question. And then another. Even when she'd planned a picnic for Marcie's birthday, she'd found a way to make her feel guilty. "You know I don't like that dressing. This is so stupid, I mean, a merry-go-round. I'm not a little girl, you know."

She knew, oh boy did she know, but she and Leo had memories of the merry-go-round, and now there was Arjay, too, and he'd enjoy it, and couldn't Marcie enjoy him even for a minute because he was here and wasn't going to go away and it was time to become at least the semblance of a family. She caught herself, mid-reverie, not reverie so much as flashback, caught herself caught up in the present tense of it, because it was past. All past. And he *had* gone away. Nothing was permanent. But the moment made her pause, because we forget that so easily, forget that what we know today may be gone tomorrow, forget to look at it and savor it and hold it in our laps. Tomorrow, we say, without thinking that tomorrow may not come. And that was the way it had to be, because otherwise we couldn't go on living, could we, not with all that responsibility clamping down like a jaw. She had to stop reliving. It didn't change the past, or the present. She needed to get out of this house more often, and the car backed into the road and then turned swiftly in the direction of Dublin and beyond, neat motion, acceleration, and the house receding in the rearview mirror, shrinking to a white patch in the distance, a place where someone lived, a place to return to, later, late at night, and she'd forgotten to leave a light on, to welcome them.

She'd forgotten to check at Jackie's, to see if the car was back, but it wouldn't be, not yet, not even if the baby had come, because he'd want to see the baby and there'd be people to call, that sort of thing. And by now Sheri would be home to relieve her mother and the boys would be getting up from their naps and she hoped that Sheri wouldn't destroy their drawings until someone else saw them at the very least. She should have left a note, but how many notes can you leave in a day?

Maybe she'd call the hospital herself, just check in, let Bob know about the pizza in case that would be helpful. Yes, she'd do that as soon as she got into town, maybe from Ted's. She was assuming that Ted would be there, just because he'd been there that morning. Stupid. She should have called. But she hadn't. She'd have to stop at the Convenient Mart at the edge of the village and make a call. Or else she'd have to plan something else to do with her afternoon. It felt like a Saturday. Errands, but nothing rigid. The whole day ahead, but still so many things to fit into it. Time did not do that in Maine, though she had to agree with Leo that if they lived there it would begin to feel just like this. It was the fact that they stepped outside of time, or outside of their version of time, that made it so attractive. Anywhere would do, as long as it was not the house on Eccles Road. Sorry, Larch Lane. It wasn't as though she didn't know her own address, just that she had liked the other address better, though there had been no number 7, just Route 2, Eccles Road, Dublin. And the letters had arrived just as regularly as they did to 7 Larch Lane, maybe more regularly, because recently they'd had a mailman who didn't like to work and he'd dumped all the second-class mail in a Dumpster seventeen miles away. Nothing much lost, but a couple of magazines she liked to read. Nothing important. Still, it was frightening to think that maybe something important could be lost, never heard from again, and you hadn't even known it was coming enough to miss it. Just something you might have done or said or thought if only you'd received it. So that all her days suddenly seemed to be filled with the missing piece that might have been hers if she could count on things in this life.

At the Convenient, the phone was out of order. At the minimart two blocks down, you had to have a phone card to use it, not just change. Finally, pulling into her regular mechanic's place, she was able to call. Ted was home, he'd be waiting, was delighted, etc., and they hung up. Delighted? What a strange word. What did he mean by delighted? She wasn't sure she'd use that word for someone you hadn't had much to do with for eight years, would be more cautious, she thought, or else far more reckless. Delighted sounded so polite, in an odd sort of way. Still, he was home, and she'd be there in forty minutes if the traffic wasn't bad, and it shouldn't be, going into the city at this hour in the afternoon. Later it could be crazy, but she'd timed this right.

Delighted, he'd said, but then he'd wondered why. Shouldn't have used that word, so generic, could be used for a deliveryman or an assignation. And this was neither. This was, well, he didn't know what this was. A surprise, for sure. Right out of the blue, the phone call from that young actress, Lucy, and Molly was back in his life as though nothing had intervened. Back in his thoughts, though quite who he was thinking of he wasn't sure. The years would have changed her, even if other things hadn't conspired to change her even more. She'd changed almost overnight, gone somewhere deep in herself. When she spoke, it had sounded too bright, a bit artificial, like a fluorescent lightbulb. A flicker, something not quite steady at the center. Too bright, and a bit brittle, as though she might break into a thousand pieces if she didn't hold herself together. A million. An infinite breakage, the kind that couldn't be mended. It had made him afraid, and he knew that when he spoke to her he didn't use quite the same tone, the same offhanded teasing. Their relationship had relied on humor—and humor failed in the face of death. So there had been nothing to fall back on, nothing to help them over the hurdle of what they somehow couldn't talk about. He'd do it differently now, if he had the chance. Build it on something more, a serious base that they could rely on. And maybe he was being given the chance. To begin it again. And what, if he might inquire of himself, was this "it" he was referring to? He knew how he'd felt, but not how she did. She had never hinted that she wanted anything more than their friendship. And maybe that was where it should begin and end, this time. Friendship. He was old enough now to know how rare a friendship between a man and a woman can be. How exciting in its own right, without the sex, without the baggage of hurt and claim and envy. Though, if he were being honest, and he seemed to be being honest, then friendship made its own claims and caused its own jealousies. He was her friend, had been her friend, and it had galled him that she had so many other friends when Arjay died. Other men, especially the musicians, who seemed to swoop down from their perches to land in the hospital waiting room, making their claims on her stoic vigil. Whenever he had come, some other man would be there, as though he had as much right to her as Ted did. He'd begun to think of them as vultures. The kind of people who give themselves a little more importance in their own eyes because they'd touched someone else's troubles. And how was he different? He was her *friend*. But what if they all felt the same way, all felt the call of friendship to be there, when she really didn't care if they were there at all?

She was remembering his eyes, the way they got

darker when he listened. And his voice, the way it seemed to quicken on the phone. Though today it had a false ring to it, strained. But that was to be expected. Still, she could remember. And soon she would see him and maybe by the time she left they would have slipped into their comfortable old shoe of a relationship, and she'd feel easy at the audition and her voice would fly again, fill the room with its old energy. Yes, she was looking forward to singing again, in public, feeling the feeling that her voice was a magnet, that every eye was on, not her, but a space just above her where the voice created the shape of their individual desires. She could sense them staring into that shape, finding its solidity, and then she'd add something, a dimension, that molded the shape into sculpture. She sculpted desire, yes, that's the sensation she had, and she wanted to feel that again, the power of it, not a selfish power, but one that energized and defined.

He remembered her voice, the way it seemed to rise above the others. It commanded attention—he'd been surprised the first time she went onstage and it had happened. Not that he hadn't seen all her potential in the rehearsals, but that it could have such an effect, he hadn't quite anticipated that. You could hear the audience grow quiet, as though they wanted to create a deep bowl in which to catch the overflow of her voice. He'd been surprised, then amazed, at what seemed to him a transformation. After that, he hadn't been able to see her in the same way. She held a kind of magic. He attributed it to the Irish, but then, that was because his name was Boyle and somewhere in his distant past there lurked the slums of Limerick. Or some such place, he wasn't sure exactly where they had come from, only where they had ended up. Boston, of course, years and years of service in Boston on his mother's mother's side, the Finnegans. And possibly the building of the Erie Canal for some male relative. Something had taken them westward. They hadn't held onto custom the way some families did, had seemed to embrace the new, the raw and unfinished. His own father was a throwback, moving east from Montana. What had they been doing in Montana? He didn't know, had never thought to ask, and now it was too late. History flowing back into the vast generic pool. They had become America; without making much of an effort, they had assimilated, and now history could only be marked by canals and dams and farmland gone back to prairie. Funny how the personal and the political intersect. He'd been just the right age for Vietnam, but his number had been high. A whole other life he might have lived, but didn't. Or one he might not have lived at all. Strange to think of it now, just when she would be coming. The way that death can pass you by, or the way a voice can hold you in its thrall, as though it contained some secret and if you could only catch a thread, you might live forever.

And then Molly was on her way, almost oblivious of the road, the car like a second body, moving easily in a familiar pattern. How many times had she come this direction, then back again to her home? Thousands, certainly. Every time she wanted to do something, this was the way she began. At the other end, there were decisions to make, which exit to take, the shortest distance, etc. But for now, there was simply one direction and she was taking it and she was not thinking about driving, but about a story her father had told her of how he had once been lost on a canoe trip in the Upper Peninsula in Michigan. There had been four of them, he and his brother James and two friends, about nineteen years old, and they'd been caught in a storm and somehow disoriented. When they pulled their canoes onto the shore of an island in the middle of nowhere, they had no idea where they were. And they'd been met by a man who had a camp and a fire and some food. He'd told them that anyone could get lost in a storm like that and set them on their way the next day. Twenty years later, her father had found an account of that incident in a book the man had written. In that account, though, her father and his companions looked foolish and the man was their savior. For twenty years, that man had been her father's savior, and now he was a self-important old fool. She wondered how others saw her, when she saw only herself as she knew herself to be. Her father had ended with his disillusion, but she half wished she had heard the story before he had discovered its published version, just to see what shape he would have given it then.

I N THE SHOWER, HE WAS WONDERING IF
the same young women would be play-
ing on Friday when he and Harvey planned to play
again. He must look old to them, he knew, but they'd
seemed to notice him. He loved the showers after the
games, maybe even more than he loved the games
themselves. The water steaming around them, their
bodies playful, somehow, younger. Harvey had said
he was a villanelle. He wasn't sure about that, wasn't
sure he wanted to be seen that way. Rather a long,
complex novel, something nearly unwieldy, or unfinished. Something with digressions and odd philosophical forays and passionate scenes with trade
unions and dirty sex. Maybe even some violence. Yes,
he wanted to be so much more energetic than a villanelle. Of course, he knew how he appeared, tidy
and average and somewhat intellectual with his
slight myopia. A bit dazed in the head, maybe. But
still, what was inside was untidy and disorganized
and full of drive. A forward motion, but just where it

was headed was still uncertain. He'd joked back that Harvey was a sestina, so predictable by the time you got to the sixth stanza that that was why he always tried to surprise him with something new. Today it was dental floss. He had discovered a new, fat dental floss that would take care of the large spaces between his teeth. There were four such spots in his mouth, he'd said. Leo wasn't sure he wanted to know all about Harvey's mouth, or about why he was a villanelle, but there it was. Harvey was his friend—and he could count on him to be exactly ten minutes late for whatever they were going to do, to wear a white long-sleeved shirt, summer or winter, to carry his gym shoes in an old plaid suitcase, to bring up, at least once, the subject of their department chairman, and to flick him with a towel when they stepped out of the shower. Every other day for the past three years, he'd flicked him with his towel. It never seemed funny or friendly or even intimate. It just was. And every time, he'd turn and catch a glimpse of Harvey's freshly dried body, his penis wagging between his legs, and he'd look away, not quite embarrassed, but trying to be more circumspect than when they were in the shower, standing nearly shoulder to shoulder, with the steam rising and nothing in the way of looking at his slippery body but the little jets of water that separated them, the wall of clear water that allowed him to stare and be stared at, briefly, before they turned their backs and reached for their towels. So when Harvey flicked him, usually on the butt, he broke some sort of unwritten code that Leo seemed to understand but he did not. Made him look again before they stepped into their clothes and became who they were in their other lives.

The highway into the city was so dull. Three lanes in each direction, so that cars stretched for miles. Crazy system, just so people could work one place and live in wholly another. Sometimes she couldn't see the cars coming in the opposite direction; they simply seemed to disappear, either close by but at a lower level, or separated from her half of the highway by stands of trees or grassy knolls. At other times, the highway seemed to be funneled into a narrow constriction, the whole system walled in between sound barriers as they passed through another posh suburb where people didn't want the noise pollution of the very artery that made their houses possible. Molly usually listened to the radio as she drove, humming along with the music, or listening to the endless talk shows, people's odd opinions on politics, or their absurd questions of Dr. Laura. Molly disagreed with Dr. Laura on almost everything, though not about having a sense of responsibility. It was just that Dr. Laura seemed so certain, so absolute, when Molly would have been more inclined to listen and to try to find a solution that allowed parents to think of their own happiness as well. Dr. Laura seemed to think that having a child meant you had to put all your own desires on hold. Molly didn't agree, felt that sometimes people fell in love, a bit the way she'd fallen in love with Leo, and that this was not a crime, not even a misfortune, certainly not something you simply willed away. So she often found herself, as she did today, talking back, saying "nonsense," saying "she has a right to think of herself, too," thinking that she'd thought of herself and that she wasn't irresponsible, not in any sense of the word. People had fallen in love, or simply had affairs, for years, for centuries. Marcie would just have to learn to accept it, too. It wasn't as though she had stolen Leo from her mother. They'd already been in the process of the divorce—though she had to admit they had been having the longest process in living memory. He'd come up to her that night in the pub, after she'd finished singing. He'd come up to her with the grey in his hair and his penetrating eyes and had said she reminded him of his grandmother. That was pretty original, for a line, so she hadn't taken it for one. Had taken him seriously from the minute he broke away from the crowd and walked toward her.

Dr. Laura was wrong about baby-sitters, too. There was nothing wrong with getting away, having some adult entertainment. She'd always felt she was lucky that they had enough money for sitters or she'd have gone crazy. Who wanted a two-year-old in a fancy restaurant? And what was wrong with wanting to go to a fancy restaurant every once in a while? No, Dr. Laura was too child-centered, too fanatic, but Molly loved to listen to the way she didn't listen. It made her feel just a bit superior, forming the answers she would have given, or the questions she would have asked in order to discern what was really at stake. And today was no exception. She was thinking about how people were almost paranoid about their children speaking to strangers (some of her best early encounters had been with strangers, she seemed to recall), when the traffic suddenly halted. Stopped dead. There in the middle of the middle lane, and nothing was moving ahead of her. And then nothing behind, as the cars filled in and stopped. All three lanes, which seemed odd, so she supposed that an accident had just happened somewhere up ahead and that soon they'd find a way to divert one of the lanes. Happened all the time.

Too bad she was stuck between those barriers. It would have been better to be somewhere else, near one of those stands of trees, if she was going to have to wait. This wall was so high, frightening really, and the heat radiated from its concrete sides in little shimmering waves. Reminded her of that one time when she was so young, twenty maybe, hitchhiking across Europe with her friend Nan. They hadn't been afraid, though now she realized there were times they should have been. Like the time in Greece when the two truckers told them there was something wrong with the engine and the two of them would have to get out so they could get the tools from under the seat. There was nothing wrong with the engine, they'd known enough to know that, and so they'd pretended to cry and pretty soon the two men got back in and drove them on through the night to the ferry. But what she was thinking of was the Berlin Wall, the way she and Nan had somehow ended up going through Checkpoint Charlie and found themselves in

East Berlin. She wondered what they had been thinking, couldn't quite recall the mood of the day, what they had wanted, adventure probably, because it was lost in what happened later. No sooner were they walking on the other side than two young soldiers, maybe twenty or twenty-two, stopped them, asking for their passports. When they fished them out of their purses, the soldiers had taken them and walked away. Of course they'd followed, weren't as naïve as all that, knew they needed those passports to get home. Followed them into a long, low building, down corridors, into a tiny room where they asked them to take everything out of their pockets and handbags, made them put everything—lipsticks, Tampax, coins—on a little table. They'd been scared, then. More scared than in Greece. They looked so young, those soldiers, too young for the machine guns they were carrying, too young to kill and thus probably why they *could* kill and they had seen pictures of people trying to cross the wall, people cut down in the no-man's-land between the wall and safety. Because they were scared, they hadn't been able to cry, but their faces reflected fear, mirrors of fear, and then the two young men had begun to laugh. Loud, friendly laughter. Two young men flirting with two young women. Nothing more. And then they'd helped them put their things back in their purses and showed them the long string of bullets on their belts and walked them back through the corridors to daylight, laughing, waving, dipping their guns in mock salute. Two young men not unlike the two of them, now that they didn't think they could kill. But they'd turned back anyway, and retreated to safety on the other side of the wall.

Odd to be remembering that day, so long ago, everything changed, the wall dismantled and shipped in little sections to places like Portland where she'd seen a piece of it last summer. Chunks of a past that contained her. That was before Vietnam, even, so nothing had happened yet to make her aware of what ordinary people could do under extraordinary circumstances. What a great thing it was to be young and unafraid. She'd always thought that experience would make her less afraid, but really it made you more cautious. Less certain.

And the traffic simply didn't move. Sat there and sat there and up ahead there were a few impatient honks that got nowhere, and every so often the clink of a car door as someone stepped out and shaded his eyes to see if he could tell what was going on. Nothing. Simply stoppage. And she could imagine the cars filling in behind and behind until she could envision the cars backed up clear to her driveway on Eccles Road, no one getting in or out, trapping them all in their little individual worlds. She wished now that she'd bought the cell phone Leo had urged on her. But she hated watching people talking on the phone as they drove. Hated thinking that they carried their days with them that way. The car was an oasis. A place where thought flowed freely, wherever it chose. She hadn't wanted to become one of them. But now it would have been handy to telephone Ted, tell him she'd be late, or even change her plans. He'd be waiting, and there was no way to get to him. Maybe, if this didn't clear up soon, she'd see if any of the neighboring cars had a phone she could borrow. Look at the way she thought of the cars as owning the phones, not the people in the cars. It was hard to approach complete strangers, impose your life on theirs. Still, she looked to either side. A truck. No good. And a bright blue Honda, with a blond woman about thirty, looking annoyed. Still, the kind of person who would have a phone. She'd remember her for later, if she needed it.

Four cars ahead, a young man, probably a teenager, was climbing onto the roof of his car. Shading his eyes. She wondered what he could see. Most likely nothing. They hadn't had to slam on their brakes, so whatever it was was probably out of sight still. She envied him his view, though, the sea of shimmering metal. A gleaming snake of cars, coiled motion waiting to move again. And then she heard the sharp stiletto wail of an ambulance. Couldn't tell whether it was from in front or behind. How would anything get there? The cars were packed in so tightly, and the walls so constricted, no real shoulders, so how could they thread their way to whatever unfortunate event had taken place? Molly hated that sound. It reminded her of hospitals. Not of the quiet of the hospital room, which had its own heavy smells and sounds that sometimes woke her in the night, its too quiet intensity. But the sounds of coming and going. Of arrival and departure. The sounds that punctuated her days when she came and went, came and went, watching, watching, watching, what no one should ever have to watch.

It would be quite a while, she knew that now, now that she'd heard the sirens and imagined their slow progress through the stalled lanes. It would be quite a while and she needed to rethink her plans. She'd have to call Ted and skip her plans, go straight to Leo's office. Or else see how Jackie was doing. She'd see Ted tomorrow. It would be all right. What should she sing for the audition? There'd be the songs from the show, of course, but they usually asked the singers to give them something they knew, something that could show the range of the voice or the depth of the feeling. It would depend on whether there was a pianist. But her best songs were sung without piano. With fiddle and flute, or nothing at all. She liked it best when the flute seemed like an echo, higher and frail, like a trail of melody, slightly lost as it followed her home. She'd choose something for the voice alone. Humming now.

> *Down by the Sally Gardens,*
> *My love and I did meet*
> *She passed the Sally Gardens,*
> *With little snow-white feet.*
> *She bid me take love easy,*
> *As the leaves grow on the tree*
> *But I was young and foolish,*
> *With her did not agree.*

*She should be here by now,* was all he could think of. It didn't take that long. He'd driven it too many times, and he knew it didn't take that long. He'd fixed iced tea, seemed like a good, informal thing for a summer afternoon. June 16th, a day he'd remember. Remember the day she came back into his life. Was it possible to fall in love at fifty? To feel like twenty when you were fifty? Because that's how he felt and that was foolish, he knew, since all he was doing was renewing an old friendship, one that had fallen on hard times. He'd feel even more foolish when she showed up and the feeling didn't persist. It was only anticipation, not love. Love was far more complex, he knew that, it was just that he suddenly felt so buoyantly alive. All day he'd been looking backwards, editing a collection of writings and historical photographs of Ireland in 1900. These were his people— all of them, since he didn't know *which* of them. There was a milkman in County Roscommon and O'Connell Street bustling with double-decker buses and the intricate chaos of a horse fair in Bantry. Steamboats and spinning wheels. But he was particularly drawn to one photograph called "Turf cutting in Connemara." In the foreground two men worked with short-handled spades on what looked like the most windswept land he'd ever seen. In the background a huge white cloud rose like a mountain, so that they stood out like cutout figures. And above the cloud was a dark sky—the darks and lights so ephemeral he wanted to warn the men in from the storm, wanted to tell them he was waiting in their future, in a bright yellow air-conditioned room in America. All they had to do was put down their spades and look up and he'd be there, waiting.

The afternoon that had stretched so sensuously before her was shrunken now, reduced to the steady minute-by-minute turnover of the car's digital clock and the wavery sense of fumes on the rise, tailpipe after tailpipe spewing its colorless gases into the atmosphere. The highway ahead was a haze of exhaust, of sun glinting on metal, ricocheting off metal in fitful sparks and harsh streams of light. Even with the air conditioner on, the car was growing warmer by the minute, the sun beating like a hammer on its roof. Molly pitied the people who didn't have air conditioners, but did they make cars without them anymore? She supposed they must, for people in Vermont or Maine or North Dakota, maybe even Seattle, places where it didn't ever get too hot for too many days in a row. With global warming, even they'd need it soon enough. She wondered about global warming, though. It certainly seemed to be happening and the theories made sense, but the statistics themselves seemed questionable, too sketchy, too recent to account for anything but possible trends, nothing definitive. It was only a few years ago that they'd been predicting a new ice age. Science, which had always seemed so immutable in her childhood, now seemed as flawed as any other discipline, as subject to whim and whimsy and manipulation as anything else. She'd shocked herself the first time she thought that, the first time she'd questioned what an expert was saying on the television, but now she found herself questioning all the time. Pertinent questions, as though the experts had put on blinders and refused to see the other side of the story. They were always so certain—red meat is bad for you, only two eggs a week—and then, a few years later, they were taking it back, eggs suddenly had "good" cholesterol, but she'd gone on eating them in the intervening years simply because her body liked eggs, sometimes craved eggs, and now it turned out that she had been smart all along. Not her, exactly, but her body's irrefutable sense of itself. First they wanted women to take hormones to prevent osteoporosis, then told them the hormones might cause cervical cancer, then found they helped prevent breast cancer, then they worried about hormones in chickens, and pretty soon she didn't care. She'd learned one thing in her lifetime; people died. People died of a number of causes and in a variety of ways and at every imaginable age, but they died. She couldn't see spending her time reading labels for the least amount of salt or refusing to eat a steak or driving all the way across town for the latest herbal tea when, really, there was more to be doing with her time, which was running out like everyone else's.

**S**HE DIDN'T KNOW WHY SHE WAS suddenly thinking of a summer morning when she was around five, probably sometime before the flood, judging by the photo she still had, the apricot tree in the background in new leaf and the flowers in the hedge—they looked like peonies in the black-and-white photo, but then in black-and-white all flowers look a bit like peonies— blooming. She is sitting on the very top of a tall stepladder, her feet resting on the step below, the fifth step. Behind her, the sky, white and fathomless. She is wearing a sweatshirt and her brown oxfords and on top of her pigtails, a straw hat. On the bottom step, seated demurely by any standards, is her friend Gail, who is probably around seven. If they were playing dress-up, Gail has certainly got the best of the deal. She is wearing a long skirt and over her shoulder is a colorful South American woven belt. On her head, too, a straw hat, bigger and in better shape than Molly's. Gail has had rheumatic fever and is newly allowed out of her house, which is why she is sitting on the bottom and Molly, her little body so sturdy and full of health, is on the very top. Odd, though, because when Molly remembers the moment without the aid of the photograph, she is always sitting on the bottom step, with Gail towering above her. She cannot remember the view from the top step, what it was she was watching so intently.

There were several moments like that in her repertoire. Moments, shaken from their continuity, that seemed to reside in a tense of their own. Her memory had always caught her by surprise, overtaken her with its intensities. And yet this particular memory seemed to float free, to be without emotion, simply to *be*. That, she thought now, was the essence of childhood. She wondered how Andy and Jacob would remember this day, the day their brother or sister was born, whether they would remember it as the day they put a bathing suit on a fish, whether it would be infused with her fragmentary presence, the day that nice woman cooked us macaroni, or whether it would divide itself from the others, become a fleeting sense of nestling into the arms of a strange woman who smelled like gardenias, or the sensation of a ball leaving the foot and crossing the grass with a life of its own.

She wondered how she'd remember this day, in the years to come. The day Leo forgot their anniversary. Or the day she rekindled something with Ted. Or the day she remembered to bring the blocks down from the attic.

She wondered if she'd remember sitting in a long stream of traffic, something unexpected that changed the shape of her life to come. Changed her plans. Diverted her from her appointed rounds. She'd felt that sensation many times, of course, the idea that if you took one direction your life would unfold uneventfully and if you took the other it would never be the same. She supposed that everyone contained a multitude, certainly a cautious and a reckless self, one who would hold back, one who would wade in.

Okay, he was thinking, what is this? This note, shoved under his office door. Not simply a notice, or it wouldn't be folded so carefully, in half and then half again, with his name, Dr. Bluhm, carefully printed on the surface. So he stooped down to pick it up, tucked it quickly into his pocket, not quite sure why he didn't open it immediately. It didn't look official. Looked, instead, personal, though it wasn't in an envelope, wasn't quite that private. The printing was feminine, he thought, at least orderly and fine, not a scrawl. Someone had taken care.

Back from tennis, just a bit of time before he'd meet Steve again at the bookstore coffee shop. In his mailbox, a note from the secretary that Molly had called. Damn, he'd hoped to get to her before she got to him, make her aware that he was thinking of her, that he did, too, think to call. So he went through the elaborate routine for his voice mail, his extension number, his password, then the synthesized voice telling him he had five new messages (which would be hers? would he have to listen to them all?) from an outside number, and four from the internal office of telecommunications alone. Those, he knew from experience, he could simply delete. He always listened to them after whatever they were informing him of had already happened. Or else they didn't apply to him at all, no matter what the administration thought. So he concentrated on the outside calls: first Molly telling him about Jackie (god, that was good news, maybe he could pop by and see how she was doing—it was only two blocks away, just past the bookstore, right on his way, really), then Marcie (her voice so impatient, when had she begun to sound so much like Sarah that it unnerved him?), then Steve, thanking him for lunch and reconfirming the later date, then Molly, then Molly again, saying she'd be coming in. He'd have to reach her to tell her about Steve, put it back an hour. They'd still have plenty of time to eat. Celebrate, she said, so she must be in a pretty good mood. They hadn't been back to that pub in ages.

But when he phoned, there was no answer, just the five requisite rings and then the whirr of their answering machine. The first time, he simply hung up. Then he decided to leave a message in case she happened to come home before she came into the city, she certainly wouldn't have needed to leave yet to make it here by five-thirty. "Listen, Mol, I've got to meet this student at five. I'll be back here a little after six, so why don't we just meet here at the office at six-thirty? Sounds good." Then, quickly shutting the door, he pulled out the note.

Dear Dr. Bluhm,

   I just wanted you to know how much I am
enjoying this class. You have made literature
come alive for me. I usually only read Stephen
King, but you have made me think there is
more I should be reading. Do you have regular
office hours, or could I come by some time to
ask you for other titles? I wish I could see the
things you see in books, like under a microscope, but maybe I'll learn how.

   *Teresa Zankovsky*

P. S. I'm still only a junior, so I'll be able to
take some of your other courses.


Teresa, which one was she? Mentally, he tallied
his morning class. It was hard to learn all their names
in so short a time. Not the blond, that was Allison.
Must be the rather good-looking dark-haired one who
sat in the middle row. Looked right at him. Adoringly,
Molly would call it, but Molly always accused him of
letting them fall in love with themselves and thinking he had caused it, rather than the literature itself.
He'd single her out tomorrow, ask her a question,
then after the class, steer her toward his office and
make an appointment when they could really talk.
He liked it when a student showed interest, even one
who admitted she only read Stephen King. It was
touching, really, that she was that honest. Innocent.
He'd draw up a reading list, careful not to start with
*Ulysses* or anything like that, a quick little run into

literature, maybe some women first, to show her that she wasn't alone. He wished he could ask this class to read *Ulysses,* would have loved to see what Steve would make of it, but it was a summer course, not enough time to take it all in, though someone had once told him that *Ulysses* was best read in one long sitting, maybe aloud, and he'd heard of professors who held marathon readings, thirty-six hours of nonstop verbal association. He was getting too old, he guessed, couldn't imagine being able to stay up around the clock, have to leave that to younger professors, too bad. But he would rouse himself to come for parts of it, he knew, just so he could participate in reading it out loud. If he could choose, he'd pick the beginning and the end. The playful Buck and Stephen, their sparring. And then, of course, Molly's soliloquy, though that would be hard to read, without any punctuation to help you get the sense, you'd always be halting and beginning again to make the sense, or else reading along in a singsong just to keep the pace, yes, that would be best. The pace of thought. He'd have to remember that for sometime when he was giving a lecture.

He liked the spark of someone looking up, looking as though she were listening hard. This was what he loved, so it seemed important to have someone love it, too. Lately Molly had accused him of putting on blinders, of breaking under the yoke of theory. Looking for how women were absent, that sort of thing. Talking about literature as though it were culture, not vision. He knew what she meant. Molly was no dummy; her own art resided somewhere between the verbal and the aural, words put to music, so that the place where she met him was in that rarefied stratosphere of sound. She read for the sounds. She read for the author's internal rhythms, not for what was said about the place of gender or politics or economics. She read for the human. That's what she would always be—the woman who reached for the human in each member of her audience. And she could ask no less of a book. That's why he was glad he'd picked up the Edna O'Brien. Just glancing at it, he'd seen that it had that rhythm of thought, that female circularity that gained a kind of momentum of its own. Had felt its confidence. Nothing to hide here, nothing absent, no, just the absolute presence of a being, fully alive to herself. He should make room for her in his curriculum. Yes, he'd spend his time in Maine working that up. He'd have to read a lot, he knew, but there was that little bit of autobiography, *Mother Ireland* he thought it was called, to begin with. He'd find in it what she had lifted into fiction.

He tucked the note back into his pocket. He'd have to make sure the dark-haired one was Teresa before he did anything else. He'd look up when he called the roll tomorrow morning, try to put faces to names now that they'd all been discussing the books and he had some other reason to remember them. Jackie— he could fit her in before Steve. Hoped she'd had the baby because otherwise all he'd be able to do was leave a note, something. Maybe flowers. He could order them at the shop in the lobby. Though that would be more expensive. So he called the secretary. "Hi, Adele, I'm wondering if you could do me a favor. I need to have some flowers sent to my neighbor who's having a baby. Could you find a florist who would deliver today or tonight? They send them home so quickly these days. Her name is Jackie Knight. Methodist Hospital. Something bright, don't you think? You choose it. But none of those cute baby vases, just something tasteful. Thanks."

And he was out, out in the fresh air again. Then back, because he'd forgotten to leave a note for Molly. He couldn't be absolutely sure she'd get his message. Taped it on his door. "Back by six-thirty. Wait for me."

And then the summer took him into it, surrounded him with its scents and sounds as he walked the two blocks toward the hospital. Long blocks, one of them a parking garage for the hospital itself, but the sidewalk was lined with flowering trees and everything looked fresh and new.

Old, she was thinking, everything looks so dusty and old, stopped like this in the middle of the highway. The treetops she could discern beyond the sound barrier looked ancient, scarred. She supposed the constant exhaust damaged them somehow. Certainly made them yellowed at the edges. She imagined the houses at the other side of the wall, their yards like neat square napkins set out along the table of the street. She imagined the children squirting hoses at each other and the young mothers sitting around the picnic table with lemonade, but that was another era, she was sure, and now those same children would be in day-care centers, in the regulated playgrounds of the day-care centers, and the mothers would be steamy in their navy suits in some corporate suite, frantic on the computer, downloading the latest statistics on whatever was needed for the day, or else staring out of the sealed windows, thirteen floors down to where they could see people walking on the sidewalks, trying to get some sense of how hot it was, whether to brace themselves for the onslaught of evening traffic, the schedule, their day to pick up the kids, and then what to do with them for supper and bedtime, maybe take-out Chinese, though the little ones didn't like it, but they could have McDonald's. That's what it had come to now, hadn't it, at least in her own neighborhood. Yards empty of children because they were elsewhere, empty of mothers because they were elsewhere, so why did they own those large yards? For the dream, she was thinking, for the dream of what they ought to be able to be. For the dream of their parents' generation, visited on them through some elaborate convocation of status: a yard and a dog and two cars and you're in.

Then the cars began to move, just a foot or two, one lane and then another, inching forward. This sorting and weaving and jockeying for position was going to take a long time. She had no idea how far ahead the accident was—if it was an accident, but what else would keep them this long—so it was impossible to predict. She'd always been interested in the way traffic could crawl past something, then instantly spring back to life, becoming itself again with the proper intervals between cars, the proper speeds. And how long it could take to sort it all out for something as simple as repairing a bridge (one lane shut down) or taking a toll (change, she supposed, was time-consuming) or even just watching something odd in the distance, like the time there had been a hot-air balloon over the highway and everything had suddenly gone into slow motion.

She was always in the wrong lane whenever anything like this happened. The other lanes seemed to get somewhere, one or two cars moving forward, while hers stood still. She decided to gauge her own progress by the maroon car ahead of her in the right lane. If it got too far ahead, then she'd know she was right, that she was jinxed, that nothing good would come of the day. But if she caught up with it, then she'd know she'd been in the right groove, that things would work out. She didn't believe in things like that, but she needed something to keep her occupied as she inched herself forward, hovering in first gear, but wishing she could just shift into second so the engine wouldn't rev so much. But when she did, she instantly realized that she wasn't going fast enough and that there was no acceleration, so she shifted down again to where it sounded too fast for its speed, if that made any sense, and it did to her ear. She needed to think about something other than the time and what she was missing by being here and the tensions she caused herself over things that couldn't be helped. Relax, she told herself, he'll understand that it was unavoidable. But he wouldn't, would he? He'd think she'd made it up. Think she was backing away from the world all over again. And she wasn't. Truly wasn't. So she hoped the accident had been big enough that it would make the evening news, or at least the morning paper, the radio—if he'd just listen to the traffic report he'd already have heard about it, but she knew he wouldn't think to listen to the traffic report, he wasn't like that, never aware that he was living in a real world full of real worries. He wasn't like that, and that was what she liked most about him. So she shouldn't expect it of him this time just because it would be convenient for her. Should she?

The maroon car had made it now to six car lengths ahead of her. It wasn't fair. Shouldn't the policeman she imagined at the other end of all this direct things evenly? If he let two or three go, then he should stop them and let her lane go, too. And the left lane still hadn't moved at all, as far as she could tell. If she removed herself and thought of it all as one large organism, it seemed like a powerful animal just waking from sleep. Flexing its muscles, flicking a tail, blinking an eye or two, maybe licking its paws. Tensing as its eyes moved over the savanna. Tensing as it waited for something to come into sight when it might spring into motion, using all its power and skill, or else settle back for an instant uninterested. Was all of life an either/or? As though every moment divided itself into the happening and not happening, the is and the what might have been. So that a ghost life followed you, branching off at every minute, replicas of the self dividing and dividing like cells, so that somewhere, in the not-so-distant past, a what-might-have-been of a what-might-have-been is going on leading a completely other life, lost in choices you yourself could not even imagine making, but might have imagined if, at some past turn, you'd opted for *or* over *either*. She'd have to get moving soon or her brain would divide, one at Ted's apartment and one at Leo's office and who knew if ever the twain should meet again? See, this waiting was really getting to her, was causing her to think things she'd be embarrassed to admit to, so she watched the maroon car as it neared the bend and was lost in the welter of traffic, swallowed in the silvery sheen of sun on the metallic river of her thoughts.

J ACKIE, HANGING ONTO BOTH SIDES OF THE bed, listened to them tell her not to push. She heard, but her body wouldn't obey. She'd been doing this too long now, something out of kilter, something wrong, though they assured her there wasn't. Just a hard, quick labor, too hard she'd heard one of the nurses saying. No time to catch your breath. But the baby wasn't coming. Damn her. She'd been difficult from the beginning, and here she was seeming reluctant, not wanting to join the only family who'd have her. Damn. Three weeks early, probably not more than six pounds, tops, so why was she harder than either of the boys had been, why this pain that wanted to rip her open? She gripped the rails again and fought the urge to push, let herself go with it the way they'd told her to, but she couldn't go with this overwhelming urge to give it all up, to simply slide back under the weight of it all and let it be over, all of it, the terrifying responsibility of yet another new life in her hands when she still didn't even know what her own was, the terrifying permanence of it all, just let it go away, let it be someone else's problem because she was done with it, done with living, the sameness of the days and the endlessness of it, given what you knew the true ending would be. And Bob was holding her hand and talking to her but she didn't want to hear what he had to say, it wasn't his body, this body writhing in pain, and it wasn't his life stretched ahead, bleached to the bone. Men could say what they would, but they didn't feel those little bodies like an appendage. Could they dissolve with them into shyness or feel the pangs of fear when the night-light went out? She had three lives in her now, hers and Andy's and Jacob's, and she didn't have room for anyone else. He could take Lynnie. She didn't want her, didn't want to have to face what she knew she faced: the sting of being female, the teasing from her brothers ("we don't want any girls in here") or her first period, the hot rush of it, or the pain of boys, the pain of their indifference, their forgetting, their putting themselves first. She had felt she could face it from the other side, with her sons, but now she'd have to relive it all and it seemed so pointless, so horrendously cyclical, so much something she'd tried to put behind her and here it was coming full force in her direction. She didn't want this baby and she didn't want to have to think about what it meant that she didn't want her. She would let this happen to her, this dying, this dark womb she was clawing her way back to, this wave of oblivion.

So when the nurse told her Leo was asking for

her, she simply screamed that she wanted no one, no one at all, certainly not Leo, not someone who had never seen her like this, sweat-riddled and pain-soaked and furious. No one. Bob had left for a minute, but he had come right back. She hated Bob, she hated June, she hated the heat and the daylight that would go on forever and she hated being who she was instead of who she wanted to be.

Having a hard time, Bob had said, and he had told Leo he might stop by later, after it was over. It couldn't be long now, Bob had said that, too. Eight centimeters dilated, but she wanted to push. Something that men might not have said to each other even ten or fifteen years ago, but now they'd been brought into the process, helter-skelter, filled with the vocabulary. But Leo wondered whether words could convey the experience. He'd been there twice, with Marcie and Arjay, and each time he'd felt more alone than at any time in his life. More in the way, extraneous, no matter how much they tried to include him. Molly had done such a good job, really, but he'd hated the way she was so heroic. Or was that the wrong word for a woman? Heroine-like? God, he hated the way he'd learned to examine all his thoughts, as though his unconscious, if there really were such a thing, could reveal hidden prejudice, ones he never thought he'd felt, but was becoming convinced were there. Molly had been so good, so actively present, that he'd felt erased. Even when Arjay was there, a quick, happy birth, he'd had to call himself back from wherever he'd been, like a tree coming into focus through the fog. A son, he'd had a son, but he felt like the man he'd been, the boy he'd been, the person he was, a self, not a father, nothing extended or expanded or whatever it was he'd thought he'd feel, just like the self he knew with a sudden, surprising turn of events. A son. But he didn't see himself in him. His eyes, his daffy expression. He saw only another man in the world, a man-child, a penis to mark him off, his progeny.

So when she'd signed without thinking and Arjay had been circumcised right there in the hospital he hadn't expected to feel such a welling of grief. Something broken. A long tradition, cut off at its roots. What difference did it make, she'd asked, and he'd realized she didn't feel it, the dipstick into the past that measured her worth against all of history. She didn't feel what he felt. She tugged forward, into the next century, and he pulled back. How could he bear the weight of this century on into the next? And she'd looked forward without so much as a backward glance. Poor little thing, she'd said, I couldn't wait and have him know comfort and care and warmth and then have it done to him. I wouldn't be able to. You'll just have to understand. He's half mine. He's part of me, too.

If he were honest, and it seemed he was being honest with himself today, he'd have to admit that she had sensed something. He'd felt as though he owned them both—his wife and his son—as though the pronoun "my" was all it took to proclaim ownership. That he should make the decisions. He hadn't once thought that she'd make such a decision. Easy, offhand, guiltless. She'd simply signed the form and it had been done. He hadn't even been there. Guiltless, because she honestly hadn't known it would matter to him. It wasn't as though he went to synagogue. It wasn't as though he practiced anything, not even really the High Holy Days, though he didn't let his parents know that, and it wasn't as though he believed in God. She'd never have married him if he believed in God. It wasn't as though he'd given her any reason to know it would hit him that hard because he hadn't known himself, until it happened, but there it was, something between them, almost from the minute Arjay was born. Something that proved, and proved again, they could never be more than they already were to each other. That he couldn't enter her skin, or her mind, and she could not enter his. I want to be her, he had found himself thinking, and she doesn't want to be me.

She wanted to be on her way, into a future that still seemed to have a shape of its own. Odd, she was thinking, inching forward, then halting again, the car hotter than ever, how writers must think of a dozen possible futures for their characters. Must not be able to stop the flow of the story even when they have put down the pen or turned off the computer. In the bath, say, or mowing the lawn, even in the middle of a party, lines, whole paragraphs, must pop into their heads, then fade again, so that there are alternative stories floating somewhere, unexplored possibilities. She'd felt that when she was reading *Waterland*—that

Graham Swift might have been able to join the histories of his characters with the larger history of the world at any point, but that he chose certain moments only to make her think of what else might have happened, how things might have been different. At any rate, she imagined a river, opaque, and a man diving into its depths. She imagined the way the water accepted him. She imagined standing on the shore, waiting for him to break the surface, shouting, shaking the hair back from the eyes, then making his way back. But the river remains unperturbed. Wherever he is, he is lost from sight, absolved of history. She imagined standing on the shore for a long, long time, waiting for the fact of his absence to make itself known, then turning away as though something had been completed. Turning back to the future you could not escape.

The car like an oven with the air-conditioning turned off. She looked at the fuel gauge, half a tank, lucky for her, because it had been almost an hour of idling. Her line moved again, this time a bit faster, as though water were suddenly going through a sluice. And then she could see what she hadn't wanted to see—the flashing lights, the chaos of lights, both sides of the highway. Too many to count. Something terrible must have happened. Something terrible on a summer day in June when, a minute before, everything had been fine. And then . . .

Molly hated scenes like this, but she had to admit she looked hard, took in the details, when she came across an accident. They startled her, the thought of something so unforeseen. And so she looked as though she could memorize what not to do, where not to be. When, of course, that was not the nature of the beast, or else they wouldn't be called "accidents." So she looked now, ahead of her to where the highway started to widen at each side of a median strip, as the lights stirred the daylight to a frenzy, wondering what had happened on such a bright afternoon. She could see movement, policemen with flares directing traffic, and a truck that had jackknifed, folded across the guardrail. And on the other side of the median, spilling into a lane going the other direction, what looked like three crumpled cars and several ambulances. More ambulances, actually, than she ever remembered seeing at once, six or seven, two of them just pulling out with their plaintive wails, their spinning sounds. They were squeezing all three lanes into one, painfully complicated, but by now there was a pattern and she could see that soon she would be passing the scene, trying to reconstruct what must have happened by whether the cars were damaged in front or behind, the skid marks on the pavement, the tangled mess of machinery.

She was frightened, in an odd kind of way, at the thought of passing so close to such destruction. It unnerved her. The very innocence of it. The way it might have been her if she had not stopped to make the phone call. That was the feeling she hated, yes, the sense that she had fooled her own fate. Closer now, she saw two stretchers, one empty, one with someone strapped in, head rigid in its harness, an IV already in place. Oh dear, she thought, oh dear, oh dear. Seven ambulances. And it looked like six or seven cars, spun out at odd angles, ripped open like cans of fruit, or crushed and tossed aside by the weight and momentum of the trailer truck.

Then there they were, three bodies laid out on the narrow strip of grass. Covered with sheets, so you knew they were bodies. No hurry to rush them into the waiting cave of an ambulance. No need for plasma or oxygen. Nothing to be done. Three sheeted forms. Were they all from the same car? Or had fate divvied them up, spread grief around? Oh! One was so small. A child. It must be a child. Oh no. And then she was past.

The policeman was motioning her to keep moving, over here, over here, now on, but her hands would not stop shaking. She held them away from her, into the sunlight splayed across the windshield, and they would not stop trembling, so fast it was almost imperceptible, like a hummingbird's wings. Her hands would not stop and her mouth was quivering. It had been a child. She'd seen enough to know. And somewhere its mother was facing a whole life without it, maybe unconscious at the hospital to awaken to the news, maybe huddled in the backseat of a police car, weeping and weeping. But she was probably hurt, so that she would have to bear the double burden of healing, and how could she possibly do it? How could she have the strength? Molly couldn't pull over because the traffic was, by now, solid and heavy as it unfolded from its narrow stream and rushed toward the city. She couldn't pull over, but she couldn't go on. Though she did. Found herself moving farther and farther away, though in a moment they were all slowing again as yet another ambulance made its way past them, heading for the hospital. There would be another, and maybe another, and she'd have to keep her eye in the rearview mirror, her ear attuned, but her hands would not stop shaking.

What had happened back there to alter the course of someone's history? Something as innocuous as a bee in the car. Or tuning the radio. Or a child kicking another child in the backseat, something to deflect the attention. Or a trucker going just a bit too fast for conditions, but the conditions were perfect. A perfect day. Or maybe nothing at all, as if a hand had passed over and nudged one car, just slightly, into another until they toppled like dominoes. Nothing you could predict, and therefore prevent. Nothing at all. No one's fault. No one to blame. And still it was tragic.

And she was alive. She'd been singing, thinking her own strange thoughts, and she was alive. It was time to think of her own life. What did she want from it? Too fragile a thing to let slip through the fingers. She was alive on a perfect day in June and her hands would not stop shaking.

She took the next exit, pulled off on a dead-end street, and sat there looking at her hands, looking at the evidence of life in her trembling fingers. She sat for a long while, she didn't know how long, but the shadows of trees began to cross her windshield and she felt a slight chill, as though the day were about to close down, though of course, it was only a premonition. Because the days were long now, as long as they ever got, and there were still hours of daylight. But the shadows turned the car a deep maroon and she looked down at her watch and saw that there would not be time to see Ted and make it to Leo's office, and she'd need to choose. She'd need to find a phone, let him know she wouldn't be coming this afternoon. Let him know that she'd chosen, though she had no idea just what that meant. She needed to find a phone to say why she was too late; what she had seen; what she had felt when she'd seen it.

Turning into a driveway, then backing out, she thought, this is someone's house, someone else's life. I pull into it briefly, a bird crossing the sky, and then I am gone. I may never come back to this street again. Yet they live here; this is where they make their own meanings. For a moment, she wished she lived in the narrow brick house with its scuffed yard and its rickety side porch. For a moment, she wanted the swing set and the forsythia bush and the green flowered curtains in the windows. She wanted such terrible taste that all it could mean was delight in being alive, in inhabiting the moment. She wanted to live on this street in this house in this moment and never to leave it. She wanted what she suspected these people had—a continuity, a place to belong.

Where was she, he was thinking. He'd opened the door at least five times, looked toward the corner her car should be rounding. Each time, he'd felt its absence stab at him, the very emptiness of the street became a reproach. Each time hc looked, she didn't appear. It didn't take half this time to get here; he knew, he'd done it so many times. Something must have happened. A change of heart. He'd have to learn not to get ahead of himself, the way he'd been doing all day, planning how he'd do it differently this time. There was no time. There was only this empty street, and even if she were to turn the corner this second, it would mean only one thing: she was here, she was coming to talk, nothing more. He'd have to learn to take things as they come. And today they weren't coming, that was quite clear. But she could at least have called. Could have had the decency to call. And then there it was, ringing loudly in his study, and he was rushing like a schoolboy to pick it up and yes, he was so sorry, it must have been so difficult, of course he didn't mind, of course he'd see her at the audition, of course they could do this another time. But there was no other time.

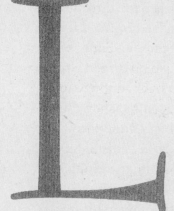EO, COMING DOWN THE STAIRS at the hospital, taking the shortcut past the emergency-room doors, suddenly found himself in confusion. Ambulances pulling in so fast that he couldn't cross the sidewalk. Seven of them, in quick succession. And a rush of assistants opening doors, wheeling in gurneys, something terrible had happened, he could see that. So many. Must have been on the highway, something large and undefinable. He'd need to watch the news tonight to see what he'd partly been party to. Seven. He stood for a while, looking up as a jet left its contrail across the clear sky, almost lazily, it seemed, crossing the horizon. Funny, when the jet was out of sight, you couldn't tell which direction it had been going, just that it had been there, left its evidence, and even that was fading, now. When he looked back, he saw two men slowly opening the doors of the last two ambulances, parked slightly to the left, no urgency about their actions. The dead, he realized, with a start. But

it was too late. No mistaking, the one by the door was so small. He wasn't going to look. Leo turned and crossed the street, headed in the general direction of the bookstore. But not seeing Jackie now meant that he had time on his hands, still nearly an hour before he was supposed to meet Steve, so he turned left toward the library. He'd pick up a book for Steve, continue their discussion of this morning, show him a contradictory opinion, have a bit of fun with it all.

Five floors down, in the stacks, he thought he saw him. His father. A man with his father's profile, because, of course, his father was in a retirement community in Florida, not here in the university stacks. Still, the uncanny sense that his father was rounding the corner as he approached, might turn suddenly and catch him unawares. Might begin his litany of how Leo had failed him, such a job he had, talking about books, making no money, not going to synagogue, not calling his mother enough, such a son. Though in truth, his real father did not say those things, simply implied them in roundabout comments, tangential remarks that were meant to sting, but not to be answered. It was true, he didn't call his mother all that often, and Molly called her even less. It was true, there was almost nothing to say to them, the ghosts of the people he'd known growing up, sturdy, practical people who knew how to survive. His father, the man he had once wanted to be, now seemed reduced to caricature. The kind of man who might haunt the underground mustiness of this library. *You always did read too much. Look, if you'll just follow me, I'll take you down two more floors to where your history begins, your origins. I'll take you to what you've turned your back on. Not that I don't like Molly, mind you, but she's taking you away from us.*

Leo hurried down the aisle, turned to see if he could find the man and dispel the uncanny sense that his father was here, in the darkness. Only two students, kissing each other so hard you half expected them to be oblivious, but when he came upon them, they broke apart guiltily and rushed off. Then, from somewhere else, a muffled giggle as their lips met again. Where did the man go? There certainly had been a man, he knew that, but now he was nowhere. The carrels were empty, except for one, dimly lit with cheap fluorescent lighting, where a young woman sat with a pile of books and what looked like a completely empty yellow legal pad. Paper due, and no ideas. Leo had seen it many times. But no elderly man, a little bit stooped, with thinning dark hair and his trousers hitched nearly to his armpits. No old man with eyeglasses, one lens so thick the frame could barely hold it. His father was in Florida, betting on the dogs, or helping with the shopping. Here, under the ground, there were only the critical minds of his own generation. A maze of his own making.

He found the book for Steve, walked back up the short flights of steps into the main lobby where he could check it out. Now he'd have to hurry, get to the bookstore in time to grab a table where they could have coffee, make it before the rush after classes, find a spot in a corner where they could really talk.

Too early for Leo's office, but what to do? There was the bookstore, of course, but she couldn't concentrate, not after the accident, not after calling Ted. Couldn't let her mind go fallow and receptive, the way she usually liked to be in a bookstore. She knew, she'd go to see Jackie. See Bob. See if Leo had been there, or maybe he'd be there and they could connect right there at the hospital. So she turned into the parking garage, collected her ticket, and made her way toward the elevator that would take her directly up to maternity. And then suddenly there was Bob, grinning from ear to ear. She's here, a girl, I knew it was going to be a girl, just over half an hour ago, six and a half pounds, black hair, a girl named Lynne. Would she like to see her for a minute, how good of her to come, Leo had come earlier but the baby hadn't been born and he had gone but now she was here and thank you for coming. And of course she'd like to see her. Jackie, tired, but smiling, in the hospital bed, and beside her a little bassinet with a tiny bundle, wrapped too tightly for such a hot day Molly was thinking, but still, they knew what to do, didn't they? She wouldn't stay long, just wanted to make sure everything was okay. Yes, she'd love to hold her, and stooping, she lifted the tiny creature to her chest, unfolded the perfect hand, watched the eyes blink and try to focus, then slip back into sleep. She's perfect, so perfect, and Molly found herself crying quietly, tears running down her cheeks so that Bob and Jackie looked away, but she said no, no, I'm not sad, I'm so happy, she's so perfect, this is our anniversary, a good day to be born.

She really means it, Jackie thought, she really is happy for me, I haven't been quite fair to her, thinking she was so distant when really maybe she just needed a friend. I'm too tired to be her friend, but later, when I have my head above water, I'll ask her over to lunch. I'm just too tired now.

Molly put the baby back in her bed, tucked her back in and patted her back, backed out of the room where Jackie's closed eyes told her she'd done all she could. She had come straight up to maternity and had not thought once about the unit on the second floor, the one where children left the world instead of coming into it. She could go down now, right past that floor, and out into daylight. She had done what she had thought she never could do. Jackie would come home to a purple sea and a fish in a blue bathing suit and two small boys looking a bit wary of their new sister, and Molly would come home to a house that would have to learn how to live again.

Leaving the car in the garage, she began walking the two long blocks to Leo's office. About a block away, down a side street, she saw a figure that looked like Leo, shadowed by one that looked a bit like Leo's father. She'd have to tell him about that when she got to his office: his body double, and a little old man with a wisp of hair, like seeing what he would become. Maybe she'd save that part, Leo was so proud of how fit he was. But you don't stop age. It sits better on some bodies than others, but in the end, the body betrays you. Better to keep the mind intact. Leo would do that, wouldn't he, with all his books? Still, sometimes she wondered what his books meant to him, the way he dipped into the middle and then began to talk about what someone might say about a particular passage. But she couldn't remember ever seeing him lost in a book, in the world of the book, so that when he looked up he'd have to blink himself back to this world, a bit shaken by its familiarity. She'd never seen that, and it worried her. Ideas were one thing, and involvement was another.

The long hallway so familiar, the place where Leo spent so much of his days, and yet today it felt alien, a place that seemed to suck in the light rather than give it back. Third door on the left. Closed. She turned the handle. Locked. He wasn't here, and now there was no one left in the office, no secretary, no way to call. And then she saw the note. Come back at six-thirty. What would she do for an hour? The weight of the day came over her. The baby-sitting. The accident. Her shaking fingers. Her silent tears. She didn't want to have to wait for Leo. She wanted him to wait for her, to know what it felt like to wait and wait, to want to be wanted. She wanted Leo to inhabit the uncertain territory where he didn't know where she was, or when she'd be back, or what she was doing. She wanted him to understand that missed connections are no connection. Nothing had worked the way she had planned. She was not arriving buoyed by a meeting with Ted, sure now that she and Leo would have a nice meal, a true celebration. She was arriving after a truck buckled across the guardrail, after the grim urgency of sirens, the sight of bodies lying neatly on the grass. And after a baby's sleep, so vulnerable. She needed to share these things now. Not later. Not after he'd met the student, whoever it might be, such a late meeting, nothing that couldn't be put off for a day so he could have an anniversary dinner, nothing that should take precedence over her. He'd clearly gotten her message, otherwise there'd be no note. He'd clearly known she was coming. So why couldn't he cancel whatever it was and be here, for her, when she needed him? Or, giving him his due, since he didn't necessarily know that she needed him right now, why couldn't he just simply be here, waiting for her, waiting for their evening to begin?

Not even a chair in the hallway so she could sit while she waited. Just a stark interior, like a hospital without the smells. With all the doors closed, it could be anywhere. Sometimes when she came, she'd peek in to see walls lined with books, tables with lamps, deep maroon carpets. A world within a world, lit from within. The offices looked as though you could step in and find solace, open a leather-bound volume and sink into its words. The waters would rise around you, but you would hardly notice. Soon the words would be floating somewhere far above, where light made the surface of the water look milky, but you had already drowned, your body pushed back and forth by the shifting currents, your hair strung out behind you, rising and falling. You were down there for the duration.

But the closed doors made her dizzy. Everyone had gone home, gone out into what promised to be a clear, cool evening, the light extending its fingers still for hours, but now, as she could see through the window at the end of the corridor, fading just slightly, as though the day had been washed and some of the color had run. A paisley day. Blurred at the edges. Not a word about where he would be, so she would be sure to miss him if she went looking. Nothing to do but wait for him, and any other day she would have waited, she knew that, but this was today, her anniversary, and she was tired of waiting.

She could have scribbled something on the bottom of his note, something to tell him where she'd be when he got back. Later, they could laugh at all the ways their lives might have been easier if just one phone call had got through. He could catch up with her. But she wasn't going to do that, she realized. And she wasn't going to wait because six-thirty would come and he wouldn't be there and then she'd be agitated and when, at ten of seven, she saw him bounding up the stairs, she'd feel such a rush of anger that it would spoil the very evening she'd been waiting all day to have. So she turned and walked back down and out of the double doorway into the pale wash of evening and back toward her car. She'd go to the pub by herself. If Leo thought to look for her, maybe they'd find each other. If not, not.

She couldn't resist the pay phone, its insistent dial tone and the satisfying clink of the quarter. She could come by now, if that was not too much bother, just half an hour, before dinner, if that was all right. And it was all right, because on this evening in June everything seemed all right and she'd sounded so needy, somehow, so disturbed by the day, but also happy. She'd held a baby, a baby girl, she'd said, who had opened her brand-new eyes.

In the car, everything seemed to fall into place. The slowly sinking sun, making spokes on the wind-shield, and the air that had freshened, as though to invite people out of doors, into the singular ending of a singular day. Still too early for the streetlights, but Molly could imagine them going on in an hour or so, to punctuate the twilight, give it an eerie glow. The streets looked enchanted, the way they some-times do after a rain, but this time they were washed in hesitancy, waiting for something to happen, some-thing that could be called an occurrence. Her car seemed enchanted, too, making the tight corners ef-ficiently, winding its way past the university build-ings, into the thriving center of the town where Ted's apartment—the bottom half of a small Victorian house, really—waited for her. She wondered if he'd painted the walls in the last few years because she re-membered yellow, a pale, evocative yellow, and she felt as though that color exactly matched her mood, her sense of the evening.

And Leo, finally settled at a corner table in the bookstore café, watching out the window for Steve's arrival, saw a red car like Molly's driving by. But it couldn't be Molly because she would be coming the other direction, toward his office, he'd have to re-member to get there on time. Then there was Steve, his dark hair flung out of his eyes, putting down his backpack and ordering a double latte. Caffeine, he was saying, to fuel him for the night. And then they were talking, the coffee going cold, as they argued the fine points. What a fine mind that young man had, too fine, really, almost more than Leo could bear. Certainly more brilliant than he had ever been, though he had something to give him, he was sure of that. But it wouldn't be long before he'd move on, find someone else to spark his interests. Leo wondered about graduate school—it could make or break this kid—its rigors, and its petty regulations. But Steve could maneuver its pitfalls, he was thinking, could fly out and beyond the ropes they would use to reign him in.

Looking at the book Leo had brought him, Steve wondered out loud about the structure of the sentence. What, for example, made Faulkner's long sentence so different from Joyce's? And Leo, being older, and presumably wiser, turned the question back on the student. So Steve began: well, in Faulkner, it takes you inside, spiraling down into an interior that knows no punctuation, or is punctuated by its very periodicity, so that it is the unending inner voice. And in Joyce, well, it's different, a different quality, maybe even an exteriority, the world coalescing around the moment, a sense that language will carry you, buoy you up, whereas in Faulkner it is where you will drown.

And Steve, being presumably younger and less wise, looked up with a question mark in his eyes, so that Leo realized he couldn't tell him he was profound since it wouldn't be good for him, but how could he challenge that, so he fished for something to provoke and came up with Molly Bloom's soliloquy. What about its interiority, its intensities? And Steve, quick to respond, said yes, of course, yes, but really, wasn't it mostly to wrap up the book, pull everything together, like glue, show that there were reasons, hidden in the spaces between words, there were human reasons for what was, in the end, myth demythologized? Leo/Socrates responded: couldn't a soliloquy do just the opposite, break things apart? His eyes are so intense, Leo was thinking, so full of the future. I am only an interval in what will be his life. I've been an interval in so many lives, maybe even in my own. Looking up, Leo saw the old man again, standing by the newspaper rack, a man not unlike his father, his trousers too high and his thin hair combed back, but without the thick glasses, the sharp exterior, clearly not his father, this man who obviously loved libraries and bookstores, oblivious to the middle-aged professor and the eager young student as he pondered which city's news he'd most like to read. Tonight's headlines, or the morning's *New York Times*? Maybe both. Leo sighed. No one to hold him accountable, not for the long line of history of which he was a part, yes, but not a participant. No, this man was not his father, not at all like him, really. A little shorter and more content, that was clear in the way he held himself so patiently, so he did not have to fear the tense, insistent voice that would tell him what he owed, and would keep on owing, that never, not in his wildest imagination, could he ever hope to repay.

Steve, looking up, saw an old man buying a newspaper. Oddly familiar, the body slightly shrunken, the hair gone thin. His grandfather, who had died last year, leaving him with the hollow feeling that he was not immortal, after all. Had made him want to embrace all of life because there was so little time in which to do it. So that this summer was just one more cog in the wheels of his ardor. A stop between stations. A day between seasons. He thought of his friend Buck, already well along on the way to making it, whatever people meant by making it. Bucks, for sure. Big bucks. And he knew he didn't have Buck's keen mind for the internal workings of the computers that churned out the country's business second by second. The software that opened the world to everything but what he found most alive in himself. He was worried that he would become an anachronism, like the professor here, someone just behind his times and almost aware of it.

A**T WHAT TIME DID MOLLY** *arrive at Ted's apartment?* At approximately six o'clock, although she was not keeping track of time, having given it up to the moment, and to the yellow walls that, in fact, had been repainted, but the same color, restful in summer, light in winter, a color that had served well over the years, with white woodwork, the contrast somehow defining the person who lived there, or so she was thinking, as she stood back to admire him after all these years, slightly older, with wrinkles at the creases of his eyes, but his laugh exactly as she'd remembered. Exactly.

### At what time did Leo arrive at his office?

Not at six-thirty, as he'd definitely reminded himself, but no more than fifteen or twenty minutes later. He had run the three blocks from the bookstore to the office, arriving out of breath, more winded than after three games of tennis, to find his office still locked, the note still taped to the door, and no one waiting.

*At what time did Molly leave Ted's apartment?*

She couldn't tell you an exact time because they needed time, eight years to fill in, well, really six, and they needed time to sit back in the pillows and simply look at each other. She was older, too, had gained some weight, gone grey in one wild streak at the forehead, striking, and her voice had changed, gone underground was what Ted was thinking, gone into subterranean depths so that when it emerged it was husky, secretive, almost seductive. And she had never been seductive, even if he had been seduced. So she couldn't say when they stood up and decided that they'd go to the pub, have dinner at the pub, and if Leo caught up with them, then he'd be welcome, but that they'd be friends forever and never waste six years like this again, because "again," that sense that it could always be done over, was running out on them.

*At what time did Leo leave his office?*

After opening the door, he waited for her to return. For once, she was later than he was. At seven, he wondered whether she had even found the note, the one he assumed she had seen, and so he dialed home. Only his own thin voice on the answering machine. But if she had come and then left, she would not have had time to get home. So he dialed again and left her a message. "Molly, if you've gone home, I'll be there very soon. I'm just going to wait here for you for about twenty minutes, then I'll start out. We'll have dinner in the little restaurant on Spruce, what do you say? Sorry we missed each other." Then he listened to his voice mail. Molly's earlier message, then Marcie's, and now another Marcie, strident, yes, that was the word for the way her voice sounded this second time around. Going to get her way. Sometimes it was sulky, but this was definitely strident. And then two more from the office of telecommunications. Two in one day. And then nothing. She knew he'd be back here, so why not leave a message? Now he didn't know whether to wait longer or to get home more quickly so they could eat. She could have left him a note. If she'd been there. Now he didn't know what decision to make. She'd said she'd take him to the pub. He could stop by there on his way, just in case she thought they were meeting there. Yes, he'd do that, because then he could say well, when he hadn't seen her here, he'd gone to the pub. That might help things a bit. Oh, and the book he'd bought her, the Edna O'Brien. He wouldn't save it for her birthday. He'd give it to her tonight, so she'd know he'd been thinking of her.

*At what time did Molly and Ted arrive at the pub?*
They do not know. They took both cars, and that meant finding two parking spaces, then meeting up again. Laughing. They were not thinking about time, but about distance, and how distance can be breached in the space of an hour. How distance does not even

exist if the other is alive in the mind, is present in the imagination. They were thinking about tomorrow's audition and how much fun it would be to work together and how much they had deprived themselves, though Molly could not think of her self-imposed exile as deprivation, since it had felt, at the time, like necessity. My brother Brian, she was telling him, asked if I wanted a priest to say last rites. My brother! I mean my father had shucked off all that religious claptrap long ago and Brian and I had hardly ever been in a church. We couldn't, either of us, say the catechism, even at gunpoint. And he asked about a priest! I screamed at him. Today he makes me laugh by telling that story, though he's careful because of course it's a story surrounding tragedy, but I screamed at him that no priest could save Arjay and that if there were a heaven, which I highly doubted, then he didn't need a priest to get him there. It's the "which I highly doubted" that makes Brian laugh. Hedging my bets. In my fury. She was telling him everything, even Arjay's death, which he had been a part of, but which she had shut him out from, and she was laughing at herself. Something had happened between eight this morning and eight this evening and she couldn't have told him what, but he was part of it, and it felt good. So she had no idea what time they arrived, just that they got there, parked their cars, entered the crowded room, found themselves a table in the corner, a table for four, in case Leo showed up, and then they began talking all over again.

*At what time did Leo arrive at the pub?*

At exactly 7:23. He looked at his watch, a digital, and he could testify that it was 7:23 exactly, though of course he could not say how many seconds. He left again at 7:31. So it took him eight minutes to look over the tables and discover she was not there, to go to the bar to ask if anyone had asked for him or left a message, and to stop in the men's room before he left. It was 7:31 because he checked his watch again, knowing that if he got home by 8:15 he'd be lucky, and they'd be having a late dinner now, and it certainly couldn't be all his fault because he'd stopped here on the way, just in case.

*What was the nature of Molly's conversation?*

A broad spectrum. Everything from the debate over chicken wings versus onion rings to religion versus aesthetics.

*What was the nature of Leo's conversation?*

There was none, except for the bartender, who had no messages. There was silence. When he left the pub, a flock of birds was just beginning to settle in a tree nearby. Small brown birds, probably sparrows, though in the rarefied light they looked black. A low, bushy tree, so that the birds seemed to be part of the leaves themselves, talking in low, twittering tones, the tree alive with their sounds. A flutter, as though they might rise of one accord, flirt with the sky once more before they came back to their appointed branches.

But they didn't; they simply scurried around within the confines of the tree, hopping here and there, ruffling their feathers, the natter of getting ready for sleep. The tree alive with them.

### Who wanted the chicken wings?

Both wanted the chicken wings. But Ted preferred the hot sauce, while Molly liked hers medium.

### Who wanted the onion rings?

Both wanted the onion rings, but Molly didn't think she ought to eat them. Ted said go ahead, live it up.

### What did Molly mean by religion?

She meant nothing. Nothing she could name. She'd felt it once or twice, and that had seemed sufficient. Once in England, when she'd heard the boys' choir practicing in the York Minster. A sound that could only be called holy. And she was certain it was more holy in practice, when it was pure sound for the sake of making sound, than it had been later in the service where it had been part of something larger, but therefore not simply itself, pure and sufficient. Once, maybe, when she'd seen a painting in a small museum. A tiny oil painting by a fairly obscure Canadian painter, but autumn had shimmered in the painting until she had wanted to walk on into those woods and wait for winter. And the Celtic cross in Ireland, the churchyard that seemed to contain all of history. Not grand, impersonal history, but the lives of real people who had come singing from the pub and now were laid to rest where they could hear the same songs floating over sea-drenched air. Though, of course, she knew they could not hear—but figuratively speaking. And one other time, when she'd heard William Stafford read a poem. Just one among many, but the hairs on her arms had stood up and she had felt the presence of something larger, something fine and simple and good. That's what she meant by religion. A high atheist, her friends had called her. Not the priests or the rote words or the prayers that always seemed to be so motivated by the moment or the bombers dying for Allah or the men weeping at the wailing wall or the pilgrims trekking up the mountains of Tibet, the mass participation in what could only, if it were to mean anything, be individual. And she certainly didn't like the New Age whirlwind of swirling skirts and crystals and cloud-filled skies, or the people who always gathered at Stonehenge as though they could pretend to know what was in the mind of ancient man, or the born-again crazies who were convinced that they could cast out the devils and sell for Jesus, Jesus, Jesus. Not that. Not anything.

*What did Ted mean by religion?*

He wasn't sure. He was, he supposed, a lapsed Catholic. That seemed to be a religion in itself. It meant you believed in some things, unthinkingly, and others you had found to be impossible. Birth control, for example, made sense. He believed that God would approve of it. Maybe that He'd invented it, since He'd invented everything. The virgin birth made no sense, but it was fun to imagine it. He didn't believe in all the candles, but sometimes, driving home late from a performance, he thanked God for his life. Not in so many words, but in the way he felt as though someone had taken trouble to keep him safe.

### What did Leo mean by religion?

Tradition. The holding together through years of doing what others had done before him. Not that he did that. But the thought that he might do that sustained him. That's why he'd managed to find the gravesite. It had taken some doing, a rabbi to make a dispensation since Molly wasn't Jewish, but he'd put Arjay into the tradition, and it had given him comfort. That had been a child, back there at the hospital, and he didn't want to think of that. He just wanted to get home safely and make things right and wake up the next morning ready for a new day. That was enough religion. A new day.

### What did Molly mean by aesthetics?

She meant what she'd answered for religion. The choir, the painting, the poem, the churchyard by the sea. And she meant more, of course. She meant the purple binding on the robe they'd found in the burial site in Siberia. Five centuries B.C., and people buried their dead in finely sewn robes, with figures of beaten gold. She meant the human impulse to decorate. Not to be decorative, but to decorate. To celebrate. To make beautiful. She meant the shape the poem had made in the air, the lines that had turned, and turned her into herself. She meant color and light and pace and tone and all the indefinable things, the things that were felt, not said. The things that were there in the books, but only in the margins. Not in the words themselves, but in the way the words went together. Yes, and Ted nodded, adding his two cents, in your songs, Molly, he'd said, you made singing an aesthetic.

## What did Leo mean by aesthetics?

He meant his conversation with Steve. He meant two sides to every question. He meant the spun-gold beauty of logic when it laid out its premises and then proceeded to prove them. He meant the physicists who found in space what they had known enough to look for. Damn it, he even meant that tree full of birds.

## What did Ted think of all this?

He thought that he was glad this woman was back in his life. Vibrantly back. Back in her own life as well, if what she was saying was the case. He was glad she had stopped to call him and that she had not been in the accident, which might have happened to her if she had not stopped. He was glad to be back in the pub full of people, to hear the band warming up, the fiddle—always his favorite—winding its way through the scales of joy and grief. He was not thinking of his future because he didn't know if he wanted to. He was thinking of this moment when the fiddle hadn't yet launched into the tune, but hinted at the tune that might be. He was thinking that he couldn't wait for the hot sauce and the chicken wings and the tangy blue-cheese dressing with the celery sticks.

*What was Molly thinking about all of this?*

She was thinking that she felt freer than she ever remembered feeling, except maybe that once when they'd all been in a boat on a river and a heron had launched itself in front of them, like a shadow rising into air, and she'd known she was there and nowhere else, right at that one moment when the shadow flew in front of her on solid wings. She was thinking that she wished Leo had joined them and that she probably should have left him a note but that what was done was done and she was going to enjoy herself. She was thinking that it was so long since she'd been to this pub and she loved this pub. She'd forgotten her life in regaining her life. She was thinking that she loved the way the fiddle made space expand so that the room seemed to deepen, allow room for the song to flow free. To cross an ocean and enter the doorway of a cottage in Beaufort. She was thinking of her uncles and her father as they fitted the pipes. She was thinking of Brian at the tip of the limb of the apple tree.

*What was Leo thinking?*

He wasn't thinking. He wasn't even talking to Arjay in his head, the way he sometimes did when he was driving. He was fighting traffic. He was trying to hurry. He was impatient. He was done with thinking. He'd been thinking all day, in class, at lunch with

Steve, even playing tennis, in the library, over coffee with Steve, and now he wasn't thinking of anything but getting home and being done with thinking.

*What did memory mean to Ted?*

It meant this moment, the way it felt familiar, as though it had happened before, and it had.

*What did memory mean to Leo?*

It meant something he wanted to do more than something he did. For instance, he rarely remembered his younger brother Stanley who had died ten years ago, at the age of forty. He always intended to remember him, but he seldom did. Memory meant that owl, standing on a branch, at the edge of the highway, backlit in the sunset. It meant his effort to hold it in his mind. This owl, this night, in such an improbable place. And it meant the squeamish feeling in his stomach when he saw a place where the guardrail had been mangled. That wasn't there this morning, he was thinking, or I didn't notice it. But now, all those ambulances, and the child. It meant not wanting to keep seeing the shape of the child. It meant trying to focus on the owl, on its solemn presence on a Wednesday night in the middle of June.

*What did memory mean to Molly?*

It meant sitting in a boat as it left the front door, hovering over the front porch that was both there and not there, there in memory, but now erased by water. Stilled water that spread in every direction, effacing the road, the garden, the strawberry plants. And yet it held them there, distinct and perfected. Almost fathomable. It meant that any time she wanted to, she could dip her hand beneath the surface and find it all over again, at her fingertips. It meant that anything she had ever felt might flood over her, the way the dull drill at the dentist's called up in her body a childhood of searing pain. And that meant that memory was to be feared as well as cherished, bringing, as it did, the palpable sense that the body could never forget its trials. Its great wrenching sobs that echoed in the empty house with nowhere to go, nothing to assuage them.

### What did they eat?

Molly and Ted ate onion rings and chicken wings. They saved room for rice pudding. Leo wasn't eating. He was driving home, thinking of an owl on a branch on the side of the road. Thinking of the long intelligible sentence of the dusk.

T WAS TRULY TWILIGHT WHEN LEO reached what he still thought of as Eccles Road. Time for headlights, the road stretched out darkly on the darker landscape. The car seemed to know where it was going, like a horse headed for the barn. It knew when to downshift on the hill just before the bend for home. Knew how to stop at the mailbox by the side of the road. Then knew how to swing into the drive, adjust itself to its narrow dimensions, shift to the left for its side of the garage. The house was dark, and the garage doors were closed. So she hadn't come home after all, or not yet. Damn. Maybe she'd come back to the office just after he'd left. He should have left a note, or a note on his note, saying he'd gone home. Damn.

Inside, the house bloomed under the natural lighting they'd installed in the kitchen. Morning again on the tiled floors and the white appliances. Morning again on the country table with the four red chairs. Putting the mail on the table, he wondered where she might be. He'd try calling the pub again, or see if she'd left him a note. Maybe the table in the hall.

He stopped to turn on the porch light, opened the door to look down the road, see if maybe one of the few cars approaching might be hers. Tucked between the door and the screen, a box, a florist's box. Inside, as he opened it, a dozen deep blue irises. The card: Happy Anniversary you two, love Brian. That's what he'd forgotten, or really not quite forgotten, but had sensed without articulating. That's why this day had seemed special every time he'd thought to think about it. So that's why she wanted to go to the pub. The night they'd met. The pub, and her voice calling over the centuries. This was too bad, thirteen years, at least he knew how many, and this was sad, some-how. It wasn't as though he'd forgotten; he just hadn't remembered to remember. Not really *remember*. She'd come home soon. Maybe he could cook something, have it ready for them. He carefully cut the stems and put the flowers into the pale pink vase, opaque, like colored milk, or the inside of a shell. He set them on the table in the kitchen and propped the card next to them. The ginger pasta on the counter, and inside the refrigerator, the smoked salmon. So she had planned something for tonight. Could he cook the pasta? It only took a minute, got sticky if you did it too soon. But he could have the water boiling. He could make salad and cut the bread.

That's Molly now, he thought, when the phone rang. But it was Bob, from across the road. Molly'd bought them all pizza, he said, and they had half a pizza left over. He was bringing it across for them right now. The baby? Oh, he thought Leo knew, thought he'd talked to Molly, a girl, a girl named Lynne, mother and daughter doing well, Leo could almost hear the grin. And he just loved the boys' drawings on their kitchen table; he understood he had Molly to thank. Oh, he hadn't realized Leo hadn't talked to Molly. She'd been there, she'd seen the baby, within a few minutes of her birth, yes, the baby had been born just after Leo left. It had been easy in the end, just a bit frustrating getting going. Yes, Molly had come and gone. She'd looked so happy, and it was so nice of her to preorder the pizzas. The boys had loved it.

So Leo had to take the pizza, didn't he, and tell Bob congratulations and that they'd check in tomorrow some time, and when would Jackie be coming home? And Bob said they weren't quite sure but he'd let him know and good-bye for now because the boys were waiting alone and he'd just popped by to bring them half a large, hoped they liked pepperoni. And it smelled so good, in its square white box, that Leo thought it wouldn't hurt to have one piece before he made the salad. Large pieces required a beer to wash them down, so he opened a bottle and sat at the kitchen table and allowed himself to feel his hunger. Lunch had been long ago, and then there had been tennis and coffee, but nothing substantial, and, he realized, he was famished. He'd eat another because she wouldn't want the pizza, would be happy with the salad he made and she could do the pasta quickly if he had the water ready. There was wine in the back cupboard, he was sure of that, and they could be festive.

Setting the kitchen table with place mats, napkins, wineglasses, the rough blue pottery dishes, he thought about how the dishes and the iris seemed to come from the same store of color. A color he imagined existed in its pure form only in France, though he had incontrovertible proof that that wasn't the case right here in his kitchen. Humming, what was that tune, one that Molly used to sing? Hummed it again, to fix it in memory, so that he could ask her the words. Greens, and endive. A salad with orange dressing, something sweet and tangy. He put them in a clear glass bowl so they would provide only their own color. He cut the orange, squeezed the juice, reached for the olive oil and pepper. Put the salad in the refrigerator, went to the front door again, looking now down an almost deserted road. Once in a while a set of headlights that turned off before they reached him. He'd catch up on the news while he was waiting.

On the screen, the highway strewn with cars. Three dead, seven injured, the anchorwoman was saying. Names withheld until notification of the next of kin. Couldn't be Molly, he thought, because they'd have caught up with him by now. Notified. They knew how to find people. He knew a man in his department who had been camping in northern Vermont and they'd found him when his brother died. His colleague still couldn't quite put the puzzle together, found there were missing pieces that the police had clearly found without him. License plates. Neighbors who knew where he liked to go. That sort of thing. At any rate, he'd been sitting around his campfire on a late August evening when a police car had pulled up and a man had gotten out and called his name. He'd been so surprised. Almost more surprised than afraid, but then he'd known it had to be bad, just for the effort they'd taken to find him. Though his family was there with him, so it couldn't be one of them. He hadn't even thought of his brother because he was the one least likely to die. But that's what had happened. Falling off a ladder. So it couldn't be Molly because they could easily have found him. The secretary would still have been there, so it couldn't be Molly. That's what he'd seen, though, as he left the hospital. The aftermath. The beginning of the struggle for the injured. And the end. It had been a child, and he hadn't wanted to see that it had been a child. Why hadn't he left a minute or two earlier? Or half an hour later? Half an hour later and he'd have met Molly and they'd have seen the baby together. On their anniversary. Though he hadn't really known it was their anniversary at the time, but it would have occurred to him, thinking of the date of her birth, it would have settled over him like insight.

So where could she be? There would have been time, by now, for her to come home. And certainly time for her to call. He'd forgotten to listen to the tape. Maybe she had called. Maybe she was waiting right now for him somewhere while he was making salad.

Yes, the earlier message, though not one he'd heard before. But nothing after she had arrived at his office, assuming she had arrived there, and nothing about where she would be or where he should come. Then Marcie's voice again, impatient, put out you could say. Sounding as though he should be there simply because she wanted him to be. Sounding as though his life was an interval in hers, and this time an inconvenient one. Then nothing. The blank silence of the unused tape, waiting expectantly for something to record. The three sharp beeps that said that's all, folks. Nothing more for you today.

If he'd stopped this morning to talk, things would all be different. They'd be sitting in the pub, drinking a beer, eating food they weren't supposed to be eating. He'd have remembered, he was sure he would have, and they'd be celebrating thirteen years. God, it had been difficult for her—for him, too, but mostly for her. He'd watched her watching him, but he didn't know what to say or do.

Molly was watching Ted watch the band. His eyes were so green, she noticed, flecked with brown, almost brackish, but gentle, listening eyes. She liked the way he responded to the music, as though he gave himself over to it. Maybe that's the Irish in him, she was thinking, really more Irish than she was, on both sides of the family, maybe it's in the genes after all. Ted reminded her of someone, but she couldn't quite place who. Not her brother, who was more straightforward, but someone. Yes, her mother's brother. Not Irish at all. But Edward had been like Ted, my god, think of their names even, thoughtful and reserved, but with that willing smile, but that wasn't it, was it, no, it was more in the manner of listening, a kind of intimacy that he established quickly and easily and then wouldn't let you pull away from. He wanted your attention, and he gave it back in equal measure. Uncle Edward was like that, too, and she missed him, not the way she missed her parents, but with a pang of realization that a whole generation had gone, was going, because James was still alive to remember the songs and the Downriver Construction Company. Funny, she hadn't thought, back then, about what Downriver meant. It had simply been a name, and now it flashed, neon, in her head. They'd named themselves after the flood, after the tree and its slow demise. She remembered the year it took to dry the wood, and then the way it was stacked in the yard, five feet high, and how once her father had lifted her onto the pile and there was a photo—Molly on the woodpile framed against the sky, her hair blowing in wisps, silky, like dandelions gone to seed, that light and fine. A black-and-white photo, but still you could see the colors of the sky and her hair. She remembered the smell of wood smoke rising into winter air. Dark red, that was the color of the smell of wood smoke. She felt as though she had known that forever.

The music lifted above the crowd, and suddenly she found herself whispering the words, fitting them to the tune. Oh, what words:

*The violets were scenting the woods, Nora*
*Displaying their charms to the bees*
*When I first said I loved only you, Nora*
*And you said you loved only me.*

*The chestnuts bloom gleams through the glade, Nora*
*The robin sang out from every tree*
*When I first said I loved only you, Nora*
*And you said you loved only me.*

She wished she'd been named Nora. Not Molly, not anything with a "y" at the end, that made her sound so silly and young when she didn't quite fit the part. Molly (or Polly or Judy or Kathy, for that matter) didn't age well after thirty, she thought, while Nora was something to grow into. An eight-year-old Nora might seem slightly stiff, but now, at fifty, it would feel solid and ready for thirty more years. She didn't like the ending of the song, the part about *our hopes they have never come true* and *our dreams they were never to be,* but on the whole the song made her feel what she'd felt the night she first met Leo, as though there were new sounds and smells and the world was reduced to two pairs of eyes, looking at their own reflections in the other. And wasn't it true—it was certainly true in almost every Irish song she knew—that dreams were never to be. They were dreams, after all, and life was hard. Everyone knew that, even today, when life wasn't so hard. Besides, Molly's dreams had always been so practical. An extension of her living. If she were working on income taxes, she dreamed a new deduction. If she were baking bread all afternoon, the loaves rose in her dreams like mountains. She never had the fun of scary footsteps, or fast chases, or even the surreal feeling of being at home somewhere you don't even recognize. Even in her dreams, her home was her home. Solid white, with black shutters, there on Eccles Road. In her dreams, the road did not change its name and life went on on Eccles Road.

Listen, even at a whisper, her voice went dusky. Carried the song across the table so full of loss that he knew he could never be at its heart. He wanted to retrieve her voice, put it in a box to keep forever. What did she do that others didn't do? He'd worked with hundreds of singers over the years, some better than she was, more adept, but no one touched you the way she did. It wasn't just that she was his friend, though that might play a small role, but that something behind the voice was valid. Was attuned to what living was meant to be. And living was loss, he knew that, too, and her voice confirmed it. Even at a whisper, he could hear its undertones.

Her voice, he thought, was like the mourning doves flying past his shade at dawn. Shadows of light, they made their brush stroke on the shade, then swooped off to land on the opposite roof. That was the closest he could come to describing it, and it didn't do, not by a long shot.

And then the man at the mike was saying something, was looking in their direction. Was saying that someone in the audience knew these tunes better than he did, that someone ought to just step right up here and show them how it was done. How did they know Molly? He hadn't told them. Someone must have known her, even after all these years away. The leader was calling out her name and looking in her direction and she was flustered, he could see that, but flustered in a flattered sort of way, blushing slightly, but with bright eyes, not the eyes that had retreated and gone dull. What would she do? He was holding his breath, not wanting to break the moment. If she sings, he was thinking, I will have lost her. But he wanted her to sing. Wanted to see her stand there with her simple composure and give the room something to take away on a Wednesday night in June, something they had never had before and afterwards would have forever, if only in the retelling, the *I once heard a woman sing and she sang only to me though the room was full and I went out into the night and nothing was ever the same after that.* Because that was what had happened to him, that night she moved onto the stage and became the world. So he was holding his breath when he saw the slight movement, the hand that reached for her napkin, and he knew she would carefully place it on the table and move toward the mike and that his world would open and close in the same instant.

Her hand moved. She rose with a smile. Walked with a smile. The room receded. They would go to Maine this summer, she was thinking, and she would learn to trust the ocean. The reverse tide at the Bay of Fundy, forcing the river to flow backwards. But next summer she would return to Ireland, find a remote place in the west where she could learn Gaelic, could begin to delve into the roots of the songs that had carried her here, to this pub, this night, this conjunction of forces that seemed to be pulling her onto the stage. The fiddler whispered to her and they began. A low growl at first, a buzz, as though a swarm of bees lived just below the soundboard. A frenzy of bow on string as she joined in the litany of exile: singing with the lead singer, "The Shores of Amerikay." And then the drum stopped and the fiddle rested on the fiddler's knee and her voice was rising on its own bare bones, in a crowded room of a crowded pub, drinks spilled out over the tables and the ashtrays full of cigarette butts and, at the bar, one or two early drunks, but even they stopped mumbling and looked up when her voice offered up its whispered promise. *Oh Danny boy, the pipes the pipes are calling.* And she called out to him, her Danny boy, the one who had never been and the one who had lived on in her mind. He was child and lover and husband and she ached for him to return. Ached that she must bide. The room was lost in her aching. She knew there were tears in her eyes, but they brimmed and receded, did not spill over but simply made visual what the sound confirmed. She sang with her heart and her heart did not empty. For eight years, her heart had been a sieve. Had let her feelings fall on through its mesh. And now it was filling, slowly, like a reservoir, and there would be sound in her, she knew, to last for years to come. To take her into the next phase of her life, which was waiting. Something was waiting for her.

**S**HE STEPPED DOWN. SHE MUST have heard the applause, but it sounded muffled, as though her ears were ringing from a head cold. It seemed like Muzak, or background noise. White noise. She'd always loved that phrase, the color of it, and it made her think of a snowy evening, large flakes drifting into the streetlight, illuminated for a minute as they fell through the circle of light, then disappearing once more into darkness. A rush of flakes, like a hive, and then black silence. She heard the people talking to her, but she didn't hear what they said. She only knew that she was alive. She had no child to leave to the world; nothing would remain after her death except the memory of songs, and she would sing them. There would be no one to hold her hand at her final hour, no one but the voice of music. How extraordinary, she thought, to be thinking of death just as I feel so full of life.

He watched her face as she came back to him. The

same face, nothing altered. The same smile. But he could feel her slipping away. At least for now. For this evening. He could see her searching out the clock on the wall. Reeling from her own revival. They'd leave now, before the delicate strands began to unravel. So he put his hand on the small of her back to steer her through the whistling crowd, steer her past the drunks who were falling toward her, past the couple who had turned to some serious groping, out the door of the pub and onto the sidewalk. As they walked past the tree near the doorway, a restlessness, as though they had disturbed the sleep of a hundred birds.

That tree, he remembered, went bronze in autumn, the leaves drooping in the breeze, rusted, but holding on. They waited until after the final rain, making a sodden mess on the ground. Slick under the wet snows of December. Tonight the pavement was clear and dry, but his feet felt as though they might slip at any moment. He pulled her to him gently. This was not the moment for passion—which might or might not come sometime later—because she'd given her passion to the song. Still, he held her close and kissed the top of her forehead and told her that her voice was, if anything, better than it had been. That he'd see her tomorrow at the audition. That he'd loved the onion rings.

And then he was gone. Or that's how she thought of it on her ride home. As though he had simply disappeared into the night, when really he had walked her to her car and closed her door carefully and told her to lock it, suggesting the safest way to the highway. She'd take it, she guessed, though her normal way was quicker. Rough neighborhood, he'd said, but she didn't know what they meant by that. She wasn't afraid, had never been afraid of things like being robbed or mugged. She knew she ought to be afraid sometimes, for her own good, but she couldn't seem to muster the emotion. There were so many more things to fear in life—things like a lonely old age, or never doing what you felt called upon to do. Never giving yourself over to the heart of it. So in the end she went her way, past the row houses where people were sitting on the stoops. Boys around ten clustered under the streetlights with skateboards or roller skates. Older girls flashed by in shorts. They probably had tattoos, she knew, but in the dark their skin looked clear and enticing. On one stoop, a man jiggled an infant up and down, up and down, holding it out awkwardly the way men do, somehow making you wish the mother would return and take it up on her shoulder.

And that was all. So how rough could it be?

Until she made the wrong turn for the feeder road and found herself on streets she half knew. In daylight, she'd know how to get her bearings, but now things looked oddly out of place. She wasn't really tipsy, she told herself, so much as overstimulated. A bit confused. There was a crowd of men standing outside a bar on a corner. Catcalls as she passed, and she was glad the light had not turned red, trapping her there where they could press forward, make themselves felt. She turned off the radio so she could be more alert. This was unlike her, this uneasiness, fed by Ted's worry, she guessed, but fed, also, by her own body tingling, the leftover desires she had nearly indulged. It should be as simple as going around the block and finding her way back to familiar territory, but, of course, there were the complications of two one-way streets. Still, how hard could it be?

There, ahead of her on the corner, two women. Maybe she could ask directions. And then she saw, or thought she saw, what they really were. One had bleached her hair until it was white, the other had dyed hers jet black. The clothes just a bit too tight, a bit too short, a bit too something. As her car hesitated, the dark one stepped off the curb, made a gesture, then saw she was a woman, quickly flipped her the finger and stepped back on the curb. Who came down these streets looking for these women for a few minutes of a night? It must be so sad, somehow, to want nothing more than those clothes and the expertise they brought with them. And sadder still for those women who, she knew from watching the *Oprah* show, were really not too different from her. Had families they loved, ambitions for themselves, but somehow had run out of steam and landed on this dark curbside, watching for the next john who wouldn't be too much of a handful. Watching for undercover cops, for violent pimps, maybe even for wives out looking for their husbands. Watching for whatever would make daylight come a little sooner and send them home with a couple hundred dollars in their pockets. They had names like Francie and Janice and Jennifer but they changed them to Staci or Lu, as if they could act the part if they believed enough, and maybe they did.

Molly could imagine whole conversations with Staci and Lu, talks that grew philosophical as the night wore on, as the beer was consumed, talks that went below the surface to where they shared a dream. Staci had two young sons and a mother who lived with her. Lu was single, but she had a steady boyfriend who liked her income. Staci was hardened, but had a heart of gold. Lu was a cynic, thought men were such assholes they deserved what they got. But it was probably her own beers talking, making her a bit bewildered, or she wouldn't be on this street instead of already on a bridge over the expressway. Her stories did not make these women more real, but pushed them back toward stereotype. She had no idea, she realized, what they would think or say.

### STACI

Did you see that broad coming our direction? Too high and mighty. Like to take her down a peg or two, push her face in the gutter some night. Like to see what she would do if she had two kids to feed.

### LU

She's probably just out lookin' for her husband, one of them dingbats who peel off a couple of twenty-dollar bills for a blow job they don't dare ask for at home.

### STACI

She looked right through me.

You gave her the finger, stupid, of course she looked
right through you.

Bitch.

So Molly opened her window slightly to make
sure her head was clear, watching the blond in the
rearview mirror as she hailed a blue station wagon,
walked over and began talking, then opened the door
and got in. A station wagon. That meant kids, the
suburbs, an ordinary life. And here he was on a
Wednesday night looking for whatever he didn't
think he had at home. She wondered, briefly, did
Leo . . . but she couldn't imagine it, he could always
probably find a student, no shortage there, and he
never went out late, so probably not. But not completely beyond the realm of imagination. And just
what did she mean by ordinary?

Sirens in the distance, growing louder, the howl of
the fire engines turning the corner. She pulled into
the curb, sat waiting as they hurtled past, two of
them, as though in pursuit of each other. The red
lights screamed down the street making it whirl in
their circular investigation. Storefronts shot back the
red flare then went dead again. The pavement re-
volved. She could see them now, two blocks ahead,
and still she hadn't pulled back out into traffic,
though there was no real traffic, just the occasional
car heading nowhere. A knock on her passenger window. Her pulse quickening. Another knock, two male

faces peering in at her, laughing. "You boozin' or cruisin'?" one of them asked. She pulled away.

Overhead, the lights of a plane blinked on and off as it began its descent for the airport. All those people up there in the night, unaware of how these individual lives were playing out here on the city streets. They'd land and walk on out into the brightly lit spaces at the gate, hug the people they'd left, or the ones they were coming to see, gather in clubby little groups at the baggage claim waiting for the startling beep beep before the bags began their circular rotation toward them. One or two would meet no one, coming into town late for an early business meeting in the morning, would stand off to one side, grab the utilitarian black bag as it came off the conveyor, and then head outside for a taxi or bus. They would watch surreptitiously as the families embraced, small children revolving around them the way children will find a pole and then swing around and around until they are dizzy. The travelers will be dizzy with fatigue and the motion of arrival. And pretty soon the conveyor belt will be empty except for one green suitcase circling and circling, looking for an owner who is either long gone or else standing at some other airport, waiting for the bag that doesn't appear.

When she rounded the corner, there they were. Fire trucks blocking the way and hoses snaking across the pavement, the wet road shiny in the night as the lights spun across its surface. And one stream of water aimed into an upstairs window, a haze of wet smoke hovering over the scene. On the sidewalk, four firemen poked at a sodden mattress and bedsprings—charred and flaccid, an ugly heap of ash and soggy cotton, reeking of whatever it is that fire reeks of. That distinctive smell. So she had to back up and swing down yet another unfamiliar street, worrying now that she had circled so much she would not regain her sense of direction.

She was not afraid, she thought, but disoriented. Somehow out of tune with herself. She felt the old skipped heartbeat of anticipation, the challenge of finding her way and getting where she needed to be. She felt her body tugged into alertness, the way she had felt just before she stood up to sing, with Ted's eyes on her and her sense that anything might happen between them. And now he was already back at his apartment, probably fast asleep by now, and she still hadn't left the city. One last turn and she'd go back to the fire to ask for directions. But there it was—friendly and accessible—the familiar route that would lead her back to the house on Eccles Road.

Behind her, the dramas of the night that in the morning would be reduced to a heap of burned rubbish, a smashed beer bottle, a blue station wagon parked at an odd angle in its driveway. She'd been protected, she knew. America—Amerikay—had offered up to her family a way out of poverty and they had somehow, miraculously, taken it. She might very well have been born in Dublin, grown to womanhood in a dirty backstreet, standing against the wall as the boys filed by, her hips hard against the dank wall and no thought of flowers on a summer night. A young man hurriedly hitching up her skirts on a rainy night in April. His hard, quick jabs. She might have been cold and wary, bred of distrust. But it had not happened to her. She could sing out its sorry tale, but it had not happened to her. Nothing had happened to her that hadn't happened to thousands, no millions, of other women. She couldn't imagine herself standing on the curb in the dead of the night, hoping the next man who came along would appear clean, even a bit shy, so she could coax him. In her most desperate moments, nothing had added up to that. She willed herself to imagine, but it stopped just short of knowing what part of her was standing back there on the street corner.

She imagined Brian sleeping in his apartment in Washington, still sweaty even though the air-conditioning was steadily humming the white noise of sleep. She imagined him sleeping the way he had as a small boy, spread-eagled on the bed in a tangle of sheets. She remembered his favorite Raggedy Andy and the way its arm had needed to be sewn back on, he'd held it by that arm for so long. And his baseball cards, filed away neatly in packets of a hundred, held by rubber bands. His baseball glove, the pocket well oiled and worked until it held the shape of a ball long into disuse. The house in Sinking Springs that stood like a sentinel, there at the end of their roaming. The flood, nascent now, as it covered his sleep, the waters creeping up so slowly that they seemed harmless, as though they could carry you downstream to where your uncles were singing. And their song could carry you back to your grandfather as he carefully made his way past the stinging nettles on his way to school. And he could carry you to the sea with its intractable pounding, and the weeping of widows when the lost curraghs washed up on the shores. The weeping of history for all its lost lives, and hers was but one among many.

She imagined Ted sleeping, stretched out on the couch in his living room, the window open to catch the breeze as the heat of the day subsided. She imagined his mouth slightly open, and his hair fanned out on the pillow. She imagined him dreaming the dark dreams that come out of nowhere: a ship tossing, or the sinking feeling of feeling your way down a mineshaft. She imagined his images and they rose up in her mind like an ogham stone, inscribed with a long-lost language that no one could translate. She imagined his yellow walls.

She did not imagine Leo sleeping, because she didn't want him to be asleep. She wanted him to be worried. She did not imagine Leo peeling away his own family's past, sinking into the soft folds of the unknowable. She did not imagine him fingering the maps of Poland and Russia, looking for the tiny place names that were tied into versions of surnames, stories that spoke of where he came from. She did not imagine what it must have taken to imagine a new country, a new language, a whole new life. She did not think that Leo went to those places in himself. Maybe in books, yes, but not in his own depths. Because books were safe, the emotions tidy between two covers, not spilling out over the edges, eating away at the core of his life. In books, where the language itself invited him down below the surface, the deep and exotic interiors of the words.

She imagined Leo at home, pacing, pacing. Like a lion caught in his cage. She imagined his bare feet, familiar, size ten, digging into the carpet as he turned and turned. She imagined him going to the front door and peering down the curves of Eccles Road to where you could see the light of a car approaching about half a mile away. Each car that came, he'd imagine would be hers. But it would disappear behind the hill only to reappear closer, more discernible, more clearly too large, or too light, or too full of people to be Molly. She imagined him as she had sometimes been, and she felt strangely full of pleasure. Yes, she had put down her napkin and stood up to sing. Nothing could take that away from her. Loathing, she was thinking, loathing rhymes with nothing. Or almost. But she did not feel loathing. She felt nothing, or next to nothing. Mouthing. Sweet nothings. Roughneck? No, too far-fetched. Soothing. That's better. Yes, soothing. And touching. She'd accept touching.

T HE HIGHWAY STRETCHED ITS END-
less miles back to Dublin and be-
yond, back to Eccles Road and Leo, because by now
he'd be home, she was sure, and probably not so
happy with her. Well, she'd see what he had to say.
She'd enjoyed herself, no matter what else happened,
and she'd been singing again. She found herself wishing he had been there, to hear that moment when life
rushed through her, because maybe that would have
rekindled what he'd lost and he would have desired
her, desired the shape of the sound, the source. She
wished he had been there, and yet if he had, would
she have stood up when the leader asked for her? Or
would she have pulled back into the shell of comfort,
the place where she knew she was safe from the very
accident of living?

She must have passed the place where the accident had taken place, and she hadn't even noticed.
Her mind ahead of her, already turning into the village, pouring herself on out onto the last three miles

toward home. She hadn't even noticed, when this afternoon she had thought she could never forget. The mind was fickle, couldn't hold onto its major events while minor ones crept in without bidding. The way she had been thinking about the flood all day, for no reason at all, except that it had lain fallow in her memory for so long that now it sprouted, every detail, the white towel they had flown in the upstairs bathroom window to call for help, the men on the stairs with their heads in their hands, the orange juice and the water seeping through the register, rising like heat in the heat of the night. The dark swirling waters of the unconscious.

The porch light was on and everything else was dark. She could see that from far away. The house grew closer, grew familiar, so that she knew her way into its rooms long before she got there. Into the upstairs bedroom where Leo lay sleeping. How could he sleep when he didn't know where she was? Or maybe he was sitting in darkness, waiting. Sitting on the side porch, maybe, where it was cool and he could look up to the stars. She'd walk in and find him there, in the dark, and he would stand and kiss her. Though, if she were honest with herself, that sounded like a female fantasy. Not like anything that ever happened, except in movies, the ones that seemed unreal from the very beginning. So she wasn't surprised, really, when she pulled her car in next to his and walked in the side door, to find no one on the porch. And no one in the kitchen where, when she turned on the light, she found an empty pizza carton and two empty bottles of beer. The table set for two, and flowers! But the card was from Brian—bless him—and for a moment she'd thought they were from Leo, the proof that he'd remembered because you can't get flowers after six-thirty, not easily anyway. In the refrigerator, she found the salad, wilting a bit now, though still attractive. On the stove, a pan of cooling water. In the dining room, another table set for two. Two missed opportunities; they'd laugh in the morning. She was too tired to dismantle them. Maybe they'd have breakfast, some champagne in the orange juice, drink it from the wineglasses. They'd draw straws, and the one with the longest could choose. His kitchen, her dining room. His blue plates, her purple ones. His red place mats, her blue ones. His cereal, her omelette. Maybe she'd choose her own, maybe his. It would depend, wouldn't it? The book was sitting beside her place. The latest Edna O'Brien. And it was signed! Oh, he hadn't forgotten. But then, and this was unfortunate, the kind of luck Leo sometimes had, she thought, because she found the sales slip, tucked into the middle by the salesgirl, and the date was today's. That didn't mean he hadn't remembered, she realized, but it meant that it was last-minute at best in the most favorable light she could give it. Not that it mattered, really. They had been married for thirteen years and surely they could weather one missed anniversary. They could go out tomorrow, or Friday. They were old enough to behave like adults. Though she felt no older now than she had that night her father plucked her from her bed and waded out into nowhere. No older than the young woman who had braved the Berlin Wall. She was not brave, she knew, and yet she felt as though she had been through a war and come out scarred, but determined. She wouldn't go up yet, couldn't go up yet, even if Leo was lying up there waiting. She couldn't bear to see him sleeping, that was part of it, couldn't bear to think he wasn't afraid and worried and almost frantic with her absence. So how could she pretend she was being adult, when what she wanted was not revenge, nothing as intense as that, but still a childish satisfaction at his uncertainty. She'd tell him she'd been with Ted, just for the hell of it. Or no, she wouldn't say where she'd been, so he'd be forced to ask. And she wouldn't say Ted, just say the pub, and that she was going to go to the audition tomorrow and that she planned to sing again. He'd wonder what had happened.

Out on the side porch, Molly looked up at the stars. She sat back on the glider and looked deep into the sky. Could all of this be about a cemetery in which she would never be allowed a grave? Where she couldn't lie down next to her own son? When she didn't even want to lie down next to him, but to flare up into the ether and be a part of whatever he was. They could have him, all those old relatives, that old, mysterious religion. They could have him, because he wasn't theirs to have. He was nothing, now. Nowhere. But he had lived and the only thing she had left was his living memory, the song of his having been here. She'd go again, some day in the far future, some time in winter, and she'd look at that little stone as though it belonged to someone else. How sad, she would think, and she would be sad, but not sad to the point of extinction.

The wind was picking up and clouds scuttled across the sky, making the stars seem to blink on and off. So far away, such other worlds. Molly knew he was up there, in their bed, but she wanted to savor the day she had had, to sort through it and discover for herself just why she had walked to the micro-phone and let her voice unravel. All day she had felt as though she were waiting, her whole life tied to her expectations of someone else. Her happiness depend-ent on someone's appearance. His phone call. His at-tention. Now she felt as though she had been waiting all these years not for Leo, but for her own self to re-turn. The self she had been the night they met, when she had seen him step forward from the crowd, that night when she'd been singing. The self she had brought from her own odd childhood. The self she had been, probably, from before birth. That baby today—Lynnie—such innocence. Made sounds like a kitten. She had forgotten. But she came formed from the womb, not entirely innocent, but something sol-idly her own already formed as she entered the world. Umbilical, her tether to the world that would shape her, and the world she would shape. Molly felt that she had been Molly from time immemorial, had carried through the birth canal these deep-felt emo-tions, a way of seeing, of thinking, a way of hearing the music that others couldn't hear. If Lynnie lived to be over 100, she would have been alive in 3 separate centuries. Maybe she'd have children and grandchildren, watching them bring their own strong selves into being. Maybe she'd do something else. That, too, would be a legacy. There was no one moment just before birth, because all moments were just before birth. Before whatever happened next, and then that became the moment before the next birth. Life unrolled like that, unexpectedly, like a truck suddenly out of control. All you could do was be there when the man asks you to sing. The words—from this morning's tune—they were so clear in her memory now. How could she have forgotten them? She heard not James or Terry or her father, but her mother's thin soprano:

> 'Twas down by the glenside,
> I met an old woman,
> A 'plucking young nettles,
> Nor thought I was coming;
> I listened awhile
> To the song she was humming,
> Glory O, Glory O,
> To the Bold Fenian men.

She wasn't old, not yet, just at the beginning of something, really. It was young nettles she was plucking, not stinging nettles.

> Some died by the glenside,
> Some died amid strangers.

But she had been there with him, had ushered him into death with her hand on his forehead. And if she died with a stranger, then what did that matter? We were all strangers, weren't we, unaware of the currents that ran through each other, the subtle weave of feelings that knitted themselves into a protective cloak. She felt as though she had taken the last stitch and put down the yarn and walked out into her life again. What would happen would happen. Meanwhile, the clouds were thickening, turning the moonlight milky, as though the milk of creation had singled out this neighborhood with its sustaining belief. She could hear the clock in the living room chiming politely. Twelve sedate notes. Soon she would stand up, throw away the pizza box, turn off the porch light, and climb the stairs to a room she had chosen in a house she had chosen to make her home. She would carefully pull back the sheet and slide in beside him. If he turned to her, she would ask him to make love to her, just once, the old way, a slow and comforting love. And if he didn't, well, maybe they could talk, facing in opposite directions, about what direction their future would take.

*

no because no she didn't call or let me know so I won't go down now even hearing her car turn in hearing that sound the garage door makes like a motor hearing the back door open so I won't go down and ask because she wants me to ask and no I won't ask let's see if she finds the book or if she thinks I might be worried if she sees the salad and knows I was trying but where could she have been all this time after eleven so she must have eaten but still it doesn't take that long to eat so somewhere someone maybe her all hot and bothered wanting to be touched but she knows and did she know the accident that I would worry though she too knows they could have found me so it wasn't her but still maybe she heard there was an accident she would let me know all the same if she wasn't trying to make her point and okay she made it because I did worry and she's right it's usually her worrying but I have to keep going don't I have to teach and keep going no time to lose myself in thought no time to dwell on the past when the future is all we have and precious little of it left but what is she doing down there all quiet and not coming up the stairs just walking around and long pauses of silence where I can't tell what she's doing only that it's not coming up the stairs there's the creak of the screen door so she's standing out there alone in the dark instead of coming up so she isn't happy I can tell that but I don't know if she's all locked up the way she was when Arjay died or simply distant and withdrawn the way she's been a couple of years now all quiet when she thinks I'm maybe interested in other people but not her and I guess I am their long legs and silky hair and the thought of their armpits or even tongues sucking me off though not why she thinks but because they don't remind me of who I was only who I am so with them there is no past I don't have to owe them anything not that she thinks I owe her much but that I owe her anyway for everything for pain for the cemetery which I should have talked to her about I know that now but then I didn't know what to do she refused to see he was dying I needed to take care of it though now I have no idea why it mattered won't be buried there myself no room besides I don't believe not really though they make me feel I owe it to them my father all sure and worried about eating a piece of shrimp as though God's shellfish could keep you out of heaven and my mother with her tight lips so that you know without even her saying that you've done something that might offend if only you knew how offensive it could be always disappointing her no matter what and Marcie too with what I owe should have called her back but didn't want to hear her voice not tonight all worried and wondering where so I didn't call but I will and it will be the way it always is her asking and me giving never the other way around until it seems I owe because I owed and that's no way to break the cycle I have feelings too she doesn't know my side of anything women don't care about men's sides they think their feelings are all that count and usually they are because we aren't so good at feelings not saying what they are but that doesn't mean we don't have them only that we can't tell them women cut right to the heart so maybe that's why this afternoon with Steve I heard him on the sentences women don't have long sentences not like those more circular but short and men go long and lucid to cover their tracks all *in the face of it/however* to make you think there's logic or underlying sense when really what it is is obfuscation of the highest order makes the world go long and slim like a railroad track though what I mean by that I have no idea still it's a simile women think in similes that's what I think is the difference like that note today under a microscope she said that Teresa who is I think the one with dark hair under a microscope no man would say it that way even writing a note because men know the sentence wears itself out like the body going soft lungs no longer elastic knees stiff and surly no not surly because knees can't be surly but there it is again thinking in a simile a bit funny to hear it in myself though I of all people should be allowed that Steve so brilliant I don't want him to know how brilliant don't want it to go to his head before his time the way it sometimes spoils them but ideas always like a sparkler those toys you push and they whirl sparks fly out red white and blue in summer air the way I used to as a child though I don't remember being a child not the way Molly does all detailed about the type of tree or name of the birds mine is all blurry like a movie out of focus maybe a Woody Allen movie out of focus he'd understand the way it blurs because the detail is too much to bear with all the ways I owe like a bar mitzvah everyone looking at you waiting for you to perform and you don't know what it means only the words that need to be sung just so because for years they did it that way I don't believe for one minute they know just how they did it way back then but what they do now becomes what they did then when you want to hold on that hard and Molly doesn't understand because her father was the one who said no no I won't and didn't go to church made his mother unhappy but she didn't have to do it herself so she doesn't know how hard it can be harder even than watching him die because with death comes history when she wanted death to be clean and hers and it wasn't only hers but she's right I haven't dealt with it though I always say she's wrong because I haven't looked hard not the way she did going down the way she did below until I thought she had drowned under all that water above her not finding her way out but slowly coming up and I still haven't gone down like two ships passing the way we didn't do it together in such separate ways we couldn't even look at each other my whole life a disappointment no I said no she knows I love her but I couldn't touch her not that way because then it would mean I had to look he was my life I don't mean literally but just that he came from my life my living body my desire for her and now I'm afraid to want her that way because I'd want him too and I can't want him because he's gone and no replacement he was only himself so much himself from day one I can't face wanting her that way all my senses so that when I come it's all for nothing better to watch those girls at tennis their thighs those little breasts with the nipples so clear under the T-shirts better my class the one with dark hair who maybe will come to my office or Steve to say the soliloquy holds it all together because they don't ask me to live inside them not that she asks but that was what I

wanted when I first saw her that night she was singing I wanted to be her song not her husband but her
song she was that full of something I had never had
that gave itself to everyone I wanted it for me I
walked over and she smiled that was where it started
not with breasts or thighs or things I look at all the
time but something inside that offered itself up to me
the breasts came later all those nights touching listening to my own blood pump into my penis until I
was so big and full with it I wanted to explode inside
her pull her over me like a second skin and touched
again until she moaned seemed to turn herself inside
out so when she moved I moved inside and it was
part of her song like mourning it was so much a loss
even before it was over because it would be over and
we knew that that's why I haven't touched her that
was a child at the hospital today we're not alone I
know that now I want to touch her but how can I say
that after all these years eight now it would have to
come from her afraid though because she's been hurt
but still how can I reach out now after everything she
still isn't coming up into our bed that has been our
bed since long before Arjay and if I touch her he will
go away just dissolve in the need of the moment he'll
be gone if I come in her again he'll cry out from that
place where I put him that I've left him there all alone
just bones for company though I know enough to
know that's not what it is all those long books by men
Melville and Tolstoy as well as Joyce so it is men who
make these things long and unbearable and women
who face them I guess though how they do it still

eludes me maybe I can think of an example not *Gone with the Wind* but something substantial that proves me wrong though I'm right in principle I can't think of one right now not like Ahab who doesn't even come in for pages and pages he takes so long to get to his obsession literal even with its seven layers because ambiguity is built on literal I always say to my classes if they can look hard under a microscope she said love hate these are names Arjay soon I am old why did I make my life a telescope instead as though the stars were down here pounding out those notes below me so quiet now I can hear it faintly chiming where is she when I need her if she comes up now what can I say she was so lovely that night like a moon shining on water I was nothing and nowhere a clean slate waiting

A PENGUIN READERS GUIDE TO

# THE HOUSE ON ECCLES ROAD

Judith Kitchen

# AN INTRODUCTION TO
## *The House on Eccles Road*

In this extraordinary debut novel, Judith Kitchen turns the tables on James Joyce's modernist masterpiece *Ulysses*. Like Joyce's novel, *The House on Eccles Road* takes place in a single day and concerns the rich and shifting inner lives of two characters named Leo and Molly. It is also set in Dublin, but in this case the time and place is Dublin, Ohio, in 1999. And, most significantly, it is told not from Leo's point of view but from Molly's.

It is Molly and Leo's thirteenth wedding anniversary, but the day begins, distressingly for Molly, like any other. Her husband, a professor of literature, sets off for the university without acknowledging the special date, leaving Molly to wonder if he will remember and what it will mean if he does not. Into this small gap of tension and uncertainty, Kitchen unfolds a story of remarkable emotional depth and psychological complexity, and also sets forth a subtle social critique. In the years following the death of their four-year-old son, Arjay, Leo and Molly have become strangers to each other, neither fully able to heal. Molly has retreated into a profound silence, ending her singing career and retiring the voice that many felt was magical. Leo has drifted away, devoting himself almost entirely to his teaching. They do not make love and rarely communicate in any meaningful way. But their inner lives are still roiling, which Kitchen reveals with a subtlety and expressiveness approaching that of Joyce himself. Around the events of the day—the birth of their neighbors' child, a traffic jam, a meeting with a precociously brilliant student, a surprise invitation to sing—Kitchen explores the fluctuating mix of memory and desire to show us, vividly and unforgettably, what it is to be human and to live in a world of time and change.

Written with a poet's attention to the sound and texture of language, *The House on Eccles Road* brings Joyce's novel forward into the present and finds within it a mirror that fully reflects the human condition in our time and place.

# A Conversation with Judith Kitchen

*1. Why did you decide to use Joyce's* Ulysses *as the scaffolding for your own novel? Why did you choose to tell your story from Molly's point of view?*

I got the original idea from reading an essay by the South African writer J. M. Coetzee, who has created a "fictive" Australian author of a book called *The House on Eccles Street*. The idea seemed too good to be relegated merely to the realm of the imaginable. I wanted to complete the task.

My own reading of *Ulysses* was thirty-five years in the past, and I decided to let it remain so. Instead, I chose to rely on my memory of what I think of as the "heart" of that great book— the way the death of Leopold Bloom's infant son haunts its pages, serving as a reminder of a lost potential and motivating his relationship with Stephen Daedalus. Joyce had already told the story from a man's point of view, and although we learn much about Molly in the final soliloquy, we know very little of what she did during the day of June 16, 1904. Her life felt like a "clean slate." I know only a little of Dublin and less of 1904, so I decided to create a modern-day, suburban Molly whose life was more compatible with my own imagination. Am I Molly? No, but her inner life is available to me. Actually, I feel that Molly created herself, as though she had been waiting a century to tell her side of the tale.

*2. References to flooding and to drowning recur throughout* The House on Eccles Road *and seem to operate on both the literal and metaphorical levels. Why are these images so potent in the novel? Why do you liken reading to drowning?*

The flood was real; that is, it happened to me when I was five years old. So the original account of the flood in the novel is almost verbatim a description of the flood that had already appeared in an essay I wrote a dozen years ago. In the essay, that was as far as I could go because that was the limit of my experience. But in the novel, I realized that the flood was the source of Molly's imagery, that it haunted her imagination. I was able to look at the flood through her brother's eyes, and then again through the expanded imagination of metaphor. For most of her life, Molly had feared drowning since it was one of her earliest experiences with death. In a sense, she is drowning in her life.

When Molly was absorbed in a book, she lost herself so completely that, in some ways, it felt like a death of the self. She became someone else. Sometimes the desire for that annihilation felt like the force of water tugging her under. By the end of the day, Leo has borrowed (or shared) her imagery. He sees her in her own terms. If the image is potent, it's because it was driven by the intensity of my own remembered experience. If there had been no flood in my life, I would probably not have invented one, but found, instead, another image to convey the quality of Molly's depths.

3. *At the end of the novel, Leo thinks of himself as "a clean slate waiting," and Molly feels that something is "waiting for her." Why is this almost mystical sense of expectation so powerful for Leo and Molly?*

Part of the magic of *Ulysses* is that it takes place in one day and yet it recapitulates the whole of a long mythology. Any one day could be that full, could resonate over time. So, yes, both Molly and Leo have expectations and hopes. They need to reconnect, or to begin again somewhere else. Leo's "clean slate" is locked in the past tense of memory—the night he met Molly. But he is willing in some wordless way to be that person again. Molly, like Penelope before her, has spent her time waiting. But this day she has acted, and if she now waits for something, it is with a different attitude and with a renewed sense of her own potential. They are on the brink—and each, in his own way, senses that.

*4. Molly and Leo both ruminate on the change of the name of Eccles Road to Larch Lane. Why is this name change significant? Are readers meant to think of the Book of Ecclesiastes in the Old Testament? Why did you choose the road's former name for your title?*

The title was chosen to pay homage to Coetzee's invention. His fictional character wrote a book entitled *The House on Eccles Street,* referring to the Dublin address of Molly and Leopold Bloom—number 7 Eccles Street—where even today visitors flock to see the setting for the book of the century. Eccles Road is more American, more rural. I moved my characters to the country and gave them a country road, then let the forces of time change even something as substantial as the geography in which they lived. So Larch Lane represents the creeping suburban sprawl that serves as the backdrop to contemporary American life. American life is fluid, undoing in an instant what took years to build. The same forces that spawn innovation can also erase history. Molly and Leo, with their separate and ancient heritages, resist Larch Lane; the name Eccles Road holds personal memory and a longer, communal history.

I've been asked this question several times and the name has nothing to do with Ecclesiastes. In some way, however, the novel is about religion—or rather, the vestiges of religion as they affect human expectation and behavior.

*5. Virginia Woolf seems almost as large a presence in the novel as Joyce. Has she been an important influence for you?*

Virginia Woolf provided the technique for this novel. I deliberately chose what I would call a "female" approach, and who better than Joyce's own female contemporary? Her work has only mildly influenced me. Reading her, I often feel as though her thoughts could occur to me. I never felt that way about Joyce, or Eliot. Their thoughts sparked my imagination, forced me into new territory. So I was fascinated that I found myself in Woolf's company on this endeavor, as though if I were to write the female version, I would need something of what she had provided to help me worm my way into the interior.

*6. Molly and Leo are very different kinds of readers. Leo is concerned with theory, whereas Molly reads for "the sounds," the "author's internal rhythms," for "the human," rather than for what is said about "gender or politics or economics." What kind of reader are you?*

I read like Molly, I can't really imagine any other way to read. So I used her to tell what it feels like to be taken over by someone else's voice. To drown.

That said, I probably also wanted to extol the virtues of that way of reading. I wanted to wrest literature back from the jaws of cultural studies and let ordinary humans explore what it is to be human again.

*7. Joyce's* Ulysses *ends with Molly's famous soliloquy. Why did you end your novel with Leo's soliloquy?*

It seemed natural to end the way Joyce ended, in reverse. But he ended with the resounding *yes,* called up from the past. My novel was more about the uncertain future. I did not want to end with a *no,* so I began Leo's soliloquy with *no,* letting him progress from there. I wanted to give Leo an inner voice, a place where he could recognize what he otherwise repressed. I wanted to find a place where he was more like Molly than he would care to admit. A place where he could confront his fears and how he hides from them. What better place than lying in bed in the dark, awake to the mind at work?

*8. Could you discuss the role of time in the novel, the way memory (or forgetfulness) influences the present?*

Time haunts me. My first book of essays had the subtitle *Essays on Time and Memory.* It seems to me that all moments are fraught with memory, that we bring to the present every aspect of the past. The five-year-old who watched the water spilling over the hardwood floors is there when the world seems fragile. When she sees an accident, when a baby is about to be born. Leo believes that to forget is to allow him to move on in the present. Molly believes that to forget is to erase, and she wants to hold on. Both are right. Both are wrong. So the novel is about the degree to which the past has a claim. After all, memory comes unbidden, so it is how memory shapes the present that counts. How the multilayered self moves into the day, and the next.

*9. One of Molly's most moving "religious" experiences comes from hearing a William Stafford poem. Which poem did you have in mind? Has your own prose writing been strongly influenced by poetry?*

The poem I have in mind is "Ask Me." The line I have in mind is "Ask me whether / what I have done is my life." It would take a lifetime to think through all the implications of that one sentence, but I am convinced that *doing* and *living* are interconnected, but not identical. My first published book was a book of poetry and I continue to review poetry regularly for *The Georgia Review.* So poetry is a dominant force in my life. In prose, I try at times to approximate the intensity and lyricism of poetry. Let's say it's a condition to which I aspire.

\* \* \*

*10. What contemporary novelists do you most admire? What are you reading right now?*

Which novelists do I admire? I'd rather say that I admire individual novels such as Graham Swift's *Waterland,* Ian McEwan's *Atonement,* Tim O'Brien's *Going After Cacciato,* Nadine Gordimer's *My Son's Story,* Edna O'Brien's *The House of Splendid Isolation,* Margaret Atwood's *The Blind Assassin.* And I'd like to push the list past novels and name nonfiction writers Richard Rodriguez, John McPhee, Mark Spragg. Nonfiction reminds us of the real world on which fiction is built. Then there's the brilliant hybrid works of the late W. G. Sebald, especially *The Emigrants.* And short stories by Mary Hood, David Huddle, Peter Ho Davies, Marjorie Sandor. And on and on, leaving out so many, loving so many. Right now I am reading Nadine Gordimer's recent book of short fiction, *Loot,* and simultaneously (because it's a book that can be read that way) Verlyn Klinkenborg's nonfiction collection, *The Rural Life.*

## QUESTIONS FOR DISCUSSION

1. Kitchen moves fluently between many different characters in the book to provide multiple points of view. Discuss the effect of this shifting in relation to the story being told. Do you feel it provides a fair and accurate depiction of what's happening? Whose voice did you find the most compelling and why?

2. The story takes place, just like James Joyce's *Ulysses,* in one day: June 16, 1999. Discuss what you thought of the action, pacing, and tension in such a short time span. Did it feel like one day? What methods did Kitchen use to expand and/or compress time?

3. There are several spots in *The House of Eccles Road* where Kitchen breaks the conventional narrative with sections in headlines

and question-and-answer format, techniques borrowed from Joyce's novel. What do these sections add to the book?

4. A forgotten wedding anniversary, the birth of a child, a traffic jam, an almost-affair—Kitchen writes of everyday occurrences, but loads them with importance in terms of Molly's thoughts and actions. How does Kitchen use ordinary, domestic acts to reach into the extraordinary?

5. Much of the book is devoted to exploring the characters' inner lives: what they are thinking, desiring, regretting, and remembering. How does Kitchen combine the internal with the external? Based on what we see of her inner life, what kind of person do you think Molly is? Are her actions consistent with her thoughts? Do her thoughts determine her actions?

6. Their neighbor, Jackie, gives birth to a baby on Leo and Molly's wedding anniversary. How do Molly and Leo respond to this birth? What meanings does it have for them? How do they respond to the death of a child in the traffic accident? How are these two events related?

7. Molly has given up singing ever since her son, Arjay, died. Finally, in the pub with Ted, she sings again. Does this moment represent a healing in Molly? Do you think she will continue to sing? What role do you think Ted, who has urged her to sing again, will play in her life?

8. What does the novel suggest about the relationship, as it is played out in Molly's life, between the creative act of childbirth and the creative act of singing?

9. Molly seems to be tired of modern life in America. She disparages cell phones, suburbia, Dr. Laura, and answering machines. How does Kitchen use Molly's memories (of her childhood, of trips

to Maine and Ireland) to help her cope with her present life? What is it that Molly really wants?

10. Discuss Leo's final soliloquy. Do you think it points to a reconciliation between him and Molly, a deeper separation, or something else entirely?

11. How are Molly and Leo different from each other? What tensions do these differences create? How have they responded differently to the death of their child? What has kept them together?

12. How important is it to know Joyce's *Ulysses* in reading *The House on Eccles Road?* What does a knowledge of Joyce's novel add to your experience of Kitchen's? What makes it possible for *The House on Eccles Road* to stand on its own?

Judith Kitchen would like to thank Anne Panning for her contribution to this readers guide.

For more information about or to order other Penguin Readers Guides, please email the Penguin Marketing Department at reading@us.penguingroup.com or write to us at:

Penguin Books Marketing Dept.
Readers Guides
375 Hudson Street
New York, NY 10014-3657

Please allow 4–6 weeks for delivery.
To access Penguin Readers Guides online, visit the Penguin Group (USA) Web site at www.penguin.com